Mother's Veil

By Shaida B. Mehrban

 New Generation Publishing

Mother's Veil

A Poem

A mother's veil so full of honour and pride
the hidden veil of the woman, embedded inside.
I need his words and not his tone
he knows of not, except it's his home
I drape the veil and hide the pain
like the torn river, hit again by the rain.
The dark and dusky side of me
became an obsessive friend that I didn't see.
It spread the blanket so warm and complete
as the dignified feeble, became the real Me.
He smears the life that I had polished clean
as he strode along on his political dream.
His smells so dear even though he's gone,
she touches his clothes as they're like home.
She hides the pain deep into her veil
as days go by and I watch her ail.
She ends her days and nights as well
as I picture her, in that living hell!
Her death and time became a deadly maze
as her eyes flickered, a slow burning haze.
The veil of the woman, who became the mother
and yet she yearned for none other than lover.
He celebrated my life, by giving me a firecracker
blast
and all he was left with was the ash and the past!!

Chapter 1

My name is Meera Chaudry, wife of Veer Singh and daughter of Shere and Rani Chaudry. I am 18 years old and my husband is only a little more than double my age. I was born in a rich family where money was power but only used by the males and since marriage, it's almost as if I have come out of my open closet only to enter another. My mother lived in that closet before me and since her haunting and unmentionable death, I started to slide my feet into her shoes and snuggle them there till they fitted well but never comfortably. Her departure that our families don't talk about is somehow driving me into the driving seat and yet I never knew how to drive but have made this journey all alone as she did. That was an election night and so is today, unregrettably there will be some winners and others losers.

As a child I have always lived with both of my parents in our bungalow named 'Rani Bungalow' right in the hustle and bustle in the ever so busy area of Delhi in India. The streets were lined with human and animal faeces, human garbage and food leftovers line the streets, faces of the slum children bewithered and yet yearning, their hair tangled together and little girls happy with their dresses three quarter lengths with lots of holes in them but they are still happy because they feel privileged to have these on their backs. They squat on the pavements and greedily look at all passers-by in search for the coin in the passers-by's pocket, but they won't always dig their hands into it. The wild dogs sniff the mosquito's and observe the swarm of flies and follow the rage of rats as they busily hunt for humans left over's and if all fails they put their head down and quietly without a bark, put one leg up and urinate on the walls of these prime properties.

Some people have these properties to look rich whereas others are filthy rich but my father was not either of them. We lived a very comfortable life and could not ask for anything money could buy. Mother couldn't buy happiness or freedom with fathers money and whilst growing up, I didn't even have a clue with what was going on in our lives except for one thing and that is, that throughout my entire carefree young life, where days were always short because there was no care in the world and nights were shorter still even after 12 hours of sleep which is never enough but, the one thing that was for sure was that mother always wore her veil.

That's how I remember her, a thin long silky scarf no matter what clothes she was wearing. She never wore it around her neck like a modern woman or on one side on the shoulders like the show off women but her style was like a royal princess, sophisticated and glamorous. Half of her hair was always covered, at times the back half would be veiled, other times it was a majority of the left side of the head and if she was wearing big flamboyant earrings then the veil was always

3

covering the majority of her right side. The veil was mother and that was me observing her as I lay here staring straight up at the ceiling and remembering her style and it's almost as if mother is here with me now. I move my head a little to make sure that her veil is still on my head just the way it was the last time we were together.

Today is the finale to my very young life, I lay slithered on to the coarse straw ropes of this heavy swinging chair, strong but not smooth like a woman's life with a man and then these timely twisted plaits twined so perfectly to hold anyone's weight just like my life, so twisted and yet on the surface so perfect and with a strong man. The big cushion underneath me is guarding me against the harsh reality of my short life and against the rope. The final straw is mine today but it was my mother's two years so, same swinging chair, slow rocking movement of our lives slowly moving on and then when the swinging stops, so will my life and so did mothers. This rocking movement is intoxicating almost as if I'm enjoying the guilty pleasure and don't want it to stop and as it slows its pace and my heart reconciles with the sad fact that it might be forced to stop. The veins the arteries and the blood vessels that have carried the hearts burden will be relieved quite soon, as I lay in the bedroom all alone with only the big golden antique mirror, witnessing the trickled blood that I have pricked out of my arms with the blunt razor blade that Veer Singh has used so often, to scrape of the hair from his armpits like the leftover food on a

4

dinner plate, not wanted.

The sand-like dull scrape against his skin gives him pleasure as he always pulls down the silver blade so precisely and whoosh, it's all gone and I have tried to memorize his motion and do it exactly in the same manner, except for the fact that when he uses the Wilkinson sword blade, it's always in a man controlled machine with a handle, so he doesn't cut himself. I took the blade from his bathroom cupboard and there was no smile or sadness, I was motionless but now I am resting, I am nearly at peace and I am smiling.

In this big bedroom fit for royalty, the scented four feet high candles parade so tall and straight like soldiers and yet there's moving life in all of them. The flames are lit on all eight of the candles, white, big and bold with wax dribbling slowly down the edges almost like my arms and legs. The flame flickers as if my last breath has blown on it and so do my eyelids as there is still life in me yet. The bright orange heat radiates just like my body heat that warms my blood.

I turn my eye to the left corner where a queen-size bed lays lazily but in its time it has seen a lot of struggling action on it, a lot of it through force and yet these sheets don't show any creased strain of the witnessed action on it as the sheets lay still and silent and so smooth like we would like life to be, but then the reds and burnt orange show danger and warmth just like the heat of the flickering colour. The four black bold posters strong and straight an exact description of the man in our lives as they all hold the bed and family together and the same posters act as the rods for the curtains as well. These match the heaviness of the room and their weight and size deter any light from getting in and yet they are never drawn and as for the orange lines they make them look intricately secret just like our lives, a short life full of aches and pains that the doctor cannot do anything about. The warm cinnamon smell of the lingering candle smell is tainted as I take a deep breath, I can, yes I can smell my own blood as it slowly trickles a small speck like a delicate teardrop onto the carpet. The carpet so clean and new just like me really, it's admired as I am by Veer Singh my husband of nearly two years but this carpet has not been here for that long, it's newer than me but then so is the news outside.

The election fever has always been the driving force in our lives as in that it controls the men in our lives and they dictate our family life. Mother always sat in her bedroom a lot and would watch Life going by and there were many moments where she would sit by the window for hours and hours and, I think that loneliness had something to do with that and I didn't have a clue about the state of her mind or the secret life that she did not share with father or I. Maybe father did know and thinking about it now, as an adult he did know but why he couldn't do anything about it or decided not to do anything about it, I couldn't even think about back then. Were her needs something that he cared very little about, was their marriage good for him as in that he held the tugging rope, but what was she yearning for and above all why couldn't he just give her the attention that she so desired, that's all she wanted, a real piece of his life, a bit more than he was sharing with her. She only had him and little old me who wasn't even an adult yet and hence the reason why she never shared anything with me.

Whilst sitting at the window we would both share the same veil, one veil covering both heads watching the outside so full of life, but here indoors it was quiet but not really peaceful, almost lonesome and we never really were a part of the 'them' outside. Many players but never us, many actions but absent from us. The happy painted face of the mother and then, there was the face where the mask is not on any more, that's the face of the married woman, her then and now me. I didn't understand it then but have come to realize since marriage that the power game was had by the men, and no matter how and when the election, this game out bid everything and everyone and any price was acceptable. Some are born winners like father, others are born losers like mother, the fortunate ones are born into a family that is powerful, others earn it and the majority are desperate to gain it and there are of course those who are the in-betweeners, some dangerous, some simple-minded and a few daring and will do anything to get a slice of the not so humble pie, gutsy individuals and yes some are simply desperate for money so will do anything in return for a few dimes or the throw away shoes that no one else wanted or for the warm worn out jacket that could see the next winter in.

As I lay stretched out but it's not a scene from a movie, its real, my legs and arms are hanging down limp and almost lifeless and I can feel the pins and needles oozing through my skin as my torso is saddled on the wide seat. As I lay here almost as if I am looking onto the long meandering narrow road with cracks and cranks whilst mesmerized with the beauty of the pain, it's deadly and sweet and somewhat numb. Its hurts from the inside but not from the outside, the dearest of all pains are from within and the fabricated pains caused by life are from the outside, I can get a bandage on these cuts and they will heal but the scar will be a constant reminder of this life of mine but without any words.

I can hear the echoing voices of women being dragged by their limp and lifeless hair threading at the bottom, they have been chosen by society to go and put their thumb print in favour to them onto the ballot paper, it's not a choice, it's a democratic choice, a simple fact that you have to go and vote for the person who is ushering you or has driven you there and even handed a few coins along the way or a few small morsels to bribe you into seeing only their name on the ballot paper. They hold your thumb onto an ink stamp and then just like the judges hard knock you print your inked thumb on the virgin paper. How naive is society and what a small price to pay, after all why should anyone really care about who wins or loses, they are all in it for themselves and are all the same, greedy and dishonest and of course the ones who are truthful and obedient to the law get no real recognition for their good deeds, but then I haven't seen that in our households at all. The smell of that worthwhile paper that they call money can manipulate minds into corruption and deviance from offers of money but in reality it's all false hopes and empty promises.

I remember that awful night so well when mother did decide to go and join her own mother in heaven but somehow, her end was everlasting for me like the open turbulent mouth of a river gushing open the wounds that will never heal as I often question myself as to why she didn't decide to stay with me, was I not worth her troubles even though I had not actually caused them. I couldn't understand two years back but I can now as I am in the same state of mind as she was and I don't have a child so I am officially alone. I do however forgive her now only because I have become a replica of her and if she could see me now she would not be happy, but then if she can go to her mother, so can I. I know its past tea time and in India this time is quite special, everyone even those who cannot afford it will have tea in the afternoon, around three or four but no one is making tea today even though it was a normal day, I had been to school in my school uniform, driven by Kaka my father's driver and in father's car, but still no tea and I don't normally make tea.

9

As always even today Kaka put the radio on and whistled to his favourite tunes, old-time classic hits of the 1960's and 70's and for me they were quite gibberish as old poetic themes didn't relate to today's society, Bollywood music with old time greats like Mohammad Rafi and Kishor Kumar playback singers of yesteryears, how wonderful that I had grown up listening to them for over ten years. Music in the background, singer a little louder and Kaka's whistling even louder straight into my ears. He always had a bad habit of looking into his mirror at me sitting at the back, it made him feel that he was in charge, he was older than me, he had authority over me and he was in the driving seat and all the while repeating 'isn't this song good', my reply was a gentle nod.

Normally the drive home from school was only ten minutes but today it had taken a lot longer and I was never allowed to walk home, Kaka dropped me off and like a regular heartbeat he was there before home time. He always waited till the big clanging school gates closed to the public and only then he would depart leaving the fat bellied free spirited man to guard the school gate and everyone in it. The world inside these gates was pretty good I was with my friends and the school system was great and that was my life as I knew it. A place where I could be myself, play, laugh, talk and do as I desired so long it was within these walls and that wasn't an issue for me, I was happy and what was there not to like?

Behind these closes gates, in our disciplined

uniforms all of the school girls looked pretty much the same from the back. Blue tops and bottoms with a white scarf which most of us, but not all, wore around our neck. Some wore it as a veil others tied it around their waist draped from the neck and of course we all had our hair plaited in a single plait or in two plaits and always parted from the middle all the way to the middle of the head, that's the way it had to be. An all girl's school, all uniformed for life, all with dark hair, brown skins and all not there for the same purpose, some to study and go on to be someone in life and probably a doctor, others just to get away from their demised households and a few who were there just to please their parents. Whatever the reason, it was a fantastic place to be.

This school was a good school, it taught English and that was the important part of being well off, your children knew English and yet the parents only knew their mother tongue. Here in Delhi parents prided themselves by saying that their child goes to an English school when in fact, it wasn't an English school but rather that they taught English, but to parents it means the same thing. We stayed within these walls until one o'clock it was home time and Kaka would be waiting in the car for me. Thinking about it now, I think it was as if life stopped when I left these gates but it didn't feel like it then, it was as if I was an individual who went to school but back at home I was my parent's child as if these two were different people.

That day, as I got into the car on the back seat

as always, Kaka was so busy listening to the music that he hardly noticed the fact that our journey was taking a long time. There wasn't more traffic or many more beggars to give money to and as always they came up to the driver and passengers and asked for an English pound, nothing less even though two fifty pence pieces add up to a pound. A pound is what they asked for and that made sense for the takers and the tourists who are always plenty here in Delhi but when they ask the regular man that, the regular person always tells them to "Push Off" and in rude terms "Piss off mate or lady". In reply to that the takers would never be rude back, they learnt the hard way and so would also change their tune and ask for rupees instead. That was the difference between tourist and locals.

Thinking back on it maybe it didn't actually take longer, maybe it was that I had a gut feeling that something was not right, I don't know but as soon as Kaka parked the car in our front drive, I quickly opened the car door and ran into the house. The princess bungalow gates were black wrought iron gates that had black metal sheets twinned in between so no one could see in but we could see out from the upstairs rooms only. Papa was already waiting in the hall and as soon as I entered, he told Kaka to wait in the car as he had to drive him somewhere. I stood still as I looked at him, he patted my head as always, an inner sense of blessing and an acknowledgement of the fact that he knew I had come in and then he stood still, came a step closer and bent a little towards me. His

12

eyes were smiling; he was in a good mood. Whenever he was in a bad mood, stressed or anxious, he may paint or spread the biggest smile but his eyes were solemn and transparent. It was as if he spent free time on making different masks for different days and yet they just didn't hide him very well.

He was a sincere man. As he looked into my eyes, his eyes twinkled as his big lips that were over shadowed by his massive moustache sealed my forehead with a big sloppy wet kiss. As he edged comfortably away I breathed in to sense his smell. It was always the same, white musk perfume oil that was what he always wore, many versions of it, but always that. It was pleasant, not overpowering or timid. Somehow it gave him his somewhat sweet personality, caring and gentle. "Off you go girl" and of course that's what I did. I went straight into my bedroom, got changed into a tight pajama, and a tight short dress on the top. It was already ironed and it was on my bed laid out. I untied my plaits and I could smell the tarnished mustard oil smell, it came from my hair as Mother always put it into my hair every morning because she said it helped my hair to grow when it was in plaits and she was always right. My hair was very long, longer than hers, when I sat, so did my hair. I took the can of Pantene hair spray and sprayed my head, not to settle my hair as the oil did that anyhow but just to rid my nostrils of that strong pungent smell and then I smoothed my hand over it. It was sticky but that was ok as well, as now I can put my head scarf on, my veil and I knew it won't come off easily, that's what I always do when she was not looking and of course it's good to mask the awful smell.

The golden-threaded veil I slid onto my head, more than half way back and as I looked in the old antique life like mirror, I remembered why today my journey was so long because now my ears could hear exactly the same commotion. I hold my veil carefully and so still on my head and the two heavy sides which dangled like the heavy drape on a lifeless mannequin and yet I was so very alive and so was the noise outside. Carefully walking away from my own image and self, I delicately place myself on the bed sofa or day bed as some call it and simply stare. No one could see me as the nets were draped so still in their ivory gold colour and the big bunched decorative curtains that never get closed, lay still on the ends along with the nutty shutters to keep mosquitoes out. Some people say that they cannot sleep if there is light in the room but as for me, as soon as I lay my head onto the pillow, the darkness within my eyes automatically closes them tight as if the blackness of the night's darkness is all in my sight.

There was nothing still outside but in here there was silence, tear drop could have been felt, a pin could have been heard but the big road full of bungalows, big high buildings, a few dilapidated and other somewhat glorious all surrounded by the heated sun but not so bright today. The sun's rays were not making so much of an impact compared to the crowds outside lining the road. Bangalore road was full of people as I look out of my veiled window, so private and yet through it I see a whole horizon of tales. There's an old man who always roams the street a few times before he finally settles in front of the one opposite us, his shaking legs within his worn out trousers, his shirt half undone because of the lack of buttons and the creases reflecting a lot of his life not just on his skin but on his shirt as well and as normal, he is there now happily sitting in his usual sitting place like the placemat on the table.

He is as regular and as same as every day, unwashed, unkept and uncared for by his society and its people and I wonder if we are those people. Do we actually have any responsibility for people out there? He doesn't care, he sits as always with his legs wide open and his shoes in tatters and I know they have walked many miles and just as well that it's the summer season, but when the monsoon rains do appear and so will the rainbow and so will he make his appearance and there is nothing that will stop him or the weather. The weather is like god I think and Steptoe is without his son. I think he does look just like step toe the rag bone man, a true image of him. Many a times I have watched this programme with Kaka and though he didn't understand the comical ethics of the programme, he always laughed when I did, whether at the comedy or just with me.

He always has his son, a firm family member with him, the one who doesn't embarrass him, answer back, treat him badly or takes anything away from him and at all remains his true friend and most of all it helps him to forget the harsh reality of his life maybe, yes his ever so faithful drink and he always says that the can is his son. What exactly does he mean by that I don't know but people know of him well and a few find peace within themselves by giving him a can of this strong friendly stuff. He sits as I sit he watches silently as I do and then there's the rest. Men pulling old men into cars, to be driven to the local polling booth and another, who is firming his feet tightly on the ground but gets a dull whack on the back of his head by an on looking policeman. The policeman takes out his baton and goes to strike but the obedient old man does as he's told.

The policeman, beer-bellied, shirt ripping where the buttons don't close up neatly and with the wild growing of chesty hair, he stands firmly with his hands folded on his back. I look at the hair on his head and I am sure it's covered with lots of mustard oil. I think that but then I'm too far to smell the mustard and anyway he is wearing a berry hat so I can't really visualize it dripping down his neck and on to his back, but then his shirt looks quite clean. His nose shines from the suns heat just like his shiny shoes but everything else in him is old. A woman, she must be at least fifty is being pulled by her white sari, a widow who has no one to protect her. She too has to go to vote and the old woman who cannot walk scrapes and straddles like an injured wolf and the men from the princess bungalow have gone with their ink pads and have tightly forced her thumb on to it and sealed her thumb like a rubber stamp on a piece of corruptive paper. She is a cripple in body but these men, so called friends of fathers are cripples in mind and soul.

Cars zooming up and down the road, lights and horns on full alert, food given out to some, spicy sticky tea with plenty of milk and cardamom randomly given to the passers-by. The fat policeman licked his lips and rubs his moustache into place with the remains of the tea stains. I can tell he had burped, his stomach has gone in and then he sighed a deep breath and slowly moves his body back into an upright plank position. In India, it's perfectly permissible to burp. Another white widow in a white sari with white hair against a thin dark body struggles to move along, but she seems to be on a wayward journey. Her white veil on her head totally seals her big wide face and her teeth nip tightly the veil on her head from one side. Her teeth closely snap the cloth like the button to a thread as she quietly tries to move along like the paddling ugly duckling yet to become the beautiful energetic swan.

But I think it may be too late for her, she is not destined to become a swan, not in this life anyhow. The fat policeman is saying something to her, he talks with his eyes on the pavement but his words to her ears, then he licks his lips with his slimy long shameless tongue, she nods her head from side to side whilst scratching her left ear with her left bewithered hand. She doesn't look as if she's understood what he intimately is saying to her, he pulls his right hand out from his trouser pocket and pulls out something and quietly stands real close to her. She stares with her empty eyes carefully into his dangerous gaze and there's a still moment there and I can sense that there is distance between them both only because of his fat belly getting in the way. Slowly, she stops scratching her ear and takes what he has just given her and slips it into her under garment. Another man leads her and she starts to follow like a puppy that needs a new home but she doesn't look like a puppy, she looks like a slow black train on a long dark journey and I'm left wondering where her destination is.

I take my scarf and chew it just like she did between my two side molars but my left teeth are slightly bigger than the right so I snap the scarf with my left teeth and I walk away from the window and look into the mirror at the girl who is wearing her scarf like a lady. It's firmly on her head and held tightly in between her teeth, strong, sharp and white. That's a good pose for a perfect picture but this is not a perfect day and there are no cameras in our house. I open my bedroom door and walk all the way down the hall to the bathroom whilst making sure that the veil draped from my head stayed exactly there.

I was desperate by now to use the bathroom as using the toilet at school was never a good choice. Whenever I did, most of the time I never sat on the toilet seat but just pretended to sit a careful squat and then rinse and flush away with just a sprinkle of water. Washing your hands with the same old pink soap and then as normal drying your hands on your own clothes, that's how it was unquestionably. The times that I did forget and sat on the seat I always came home feeling very itchy and always took a shower as soon as I got home, but today I didn't need to so instead, I headed straight to Mother's bedroom.

Mother's room door was closed as normal and as I gently paced myself towards her door which was a few doors away from the bathroom. I always, always had to knock because often father would be in there too and I didn't want to disturb anything and I had done so on many memorable occasions. There would be gentle rustling of bed sheets, fluffing up of pillows and slight dull clearing of the dry throat and the look on the two adults faces when they did eventually speak with just the utter of a few words "Yes dear". Both of them would keep looking down and then father slightly gazing his look out of the window and then quite slyly bringing his gaze down towards the bedroom door. Mother so predictable, would always fumble through the open wardrobe, opening and shutting and really just taking the focus onto the small items of clothing.

I know and she knew that she wasn't looking for anything but for her own dignity and she wouldn't find it in her wardrobe. Dignity lived within her not on the shelves of the big wardrobe. She felt uncomfortable therefore she didn't want to meet my gaze for as long as father stood in the room but when he did leave, she gathered herself, as for him, he would slowly start talking to me asking me to come in and sit down and the repeating of the words "What's up girl?" and then whilst still looking down he would shut the wooden shutters in the window which were just behind the nets. He would start by saying "Well, I'll see you downstairs girls." That was his queue to leave almost as if he was getting permission from me to leave his own bedroom. As for mother, she would then start nit picking about where things should be placed and then would gently add she will tidy up later and father must be waiting for them both downstairs and without further ado, we leave the room together to go and join Father downstairs.

Once downstairs, the nervousness on her part and his uneasiness would all be dissolved like the tablet that's been thrown into the water, first it's cloudy and then it becomes clear. Normal routine begun and this was everyday life, a routine we were used to and liked, it was our individual way of life. Kaka would get the milk from the milkman at the gate at the crack of dawn and even though I would normally always be in bed, then I could hear his whistling from my open windows followed by his loud words "Thank you, thank you" whether it was for the milkman or the paper boy or the breakfast rusk man or indeed any other dealer from the egg man to the fresh bread boy.

Life here was a real routine and the routine was

full of boys out to make their money and it did feel so good because people were forever coming and in this big house, even though there weren't many people, but the outside people made me feel that I was at home and not isolated. Even if nothing else, I could happily just watch life out of my window all day long. I would always be served breakfast by Mother and Father always ate this meal with us whilst observing, eating and reading the newspaper and mother as always trying to run around him trying hard to please him. All day long I would be at school and Kaka would drop me to school and home as well, I would get changed and go into Mother's room. She was always there at that time and at times Father would also be there with her.

Today is another day as I know that he left when I came home. I am now standing outside her room waiting to hear her fluttering feet or her echoing voice on the telephone, or even an inner knowledge of knowing that she is busily looking at or through the clothes with the wardrobe door wide open and her fingers flicking like a butterfly and so was her mind but a million miles away. She is a parent and she never came to greet me and nor did he ever when I came from school and yet, I cannot say that she didn't love me but somehow our relationship resembled hers with her parents. I know they were dead now and even though they both passed away quite suddenly a couple of years ago she seemed not to have been rocked or even stirred by their death, almost as if, they were dead for her since marriage, but they weren't and she seemed to have moved from that life to this married life and yet she never spoke about the life before father came into it but why am I thinking of the dead now, why now and why today of all days.

I do have slight memories of about them as she talked to them I know and yet they visited a few times when I was very young but in the last few years I have not seen them what so ever and any conversation that I overheard was always civil. On the surface she showed no emotion for the people that she hardly ever saw and yet they were her real parents and yet the truth be known, she hid a lot of deep embedded pain. She always respected them and that's the important word, but that was only half of the missing puzzle because there was so much love for them that she didn't want to talk about. She recalled a little bit of her life with them but would skim over before the foundation was even laid and it goes on and so did she. That part of her life was so dear to her that she could never find the right words to ever explore the pain that was so deep that even I could not find the tools to open up that space that was just her's alone, but why? It was as mysterious as her and if I ever asked father, he would always say that I would have to ask Mother, but then it didn't really affect me any how!

"Ma, can I come in, I have knocked and knocked so now I am just coming in" but still knock again and that turns in to another knock and then in a sheepish sly kind of way knowing that she is alone, my right hand quietly feels the nutty pine door frame, so rough like father and yet the delicacy of the smooth like her and both of these together make this door and my life as well. Many doors in this bungalow which is not all on the one floor as you would think and all the doors have something to say and many tales to tell. This bungalow is antique and quite prestigious and has all the marks of a family home and you could imagine guards standing outside every door with perfectly pressed trousers and black moustaches shining and a slight curl at the end as if they, along with the trousers have been freshly pressed before facing the day and the stern look of the man had by them but alas that is the wrong picture because there are no guards here at all and still mother continuous to give cool vibes, no cold smiles from the men and yet she seems to have it hidden underneath her own, no visible cracks on the bungalow and yet she was broken in some way, lots and lots of talking between us all and yet no satisfaction underneath her face. The strong lingering of laughter and yet mother could not return half of it, oh yes, on the surface, it was all grand but if I scratched her life along the grains like the dining table, there would be many bitter tales untold like the food that never really comes off the table in spite of being cleaned daily. I will collect them later.

I collect my thoughts again whilst tapping against the door for the last time and then I peer my head through the tiny gap and all I see is tranquility and silence and my heart feels peaceful as I enter and there she was , all stretched out on her favourite piece of furniture in her room. A real princess, just like this bungalow, her burnt red-coloured silken sari with delicate strands of tarnished brass threads, twinned into the expensive lushes silk whilst at the ends the sari cloth is draped onto the side of her head. Her left ear covered and the right bore the constant knocking and now burdened with her long very expensive pearl earrings, so long that they touch her neck and her long jet black hair with ripples of shape in them and dragging on the floor. Her arms thrown beside her head and legs dangling down with her feet firmly on the flower embossed carpet. Her toenails still perfectly polished with red brick nail varnish and her slender feet filled with orange aromatic colours of the ever so confusing henna and its vibrancy. She wore her anklet as always and it sits lazily sleeping all the while on her skin.

Her hands matched her toes, same red brick nail polish and hand creases pressed out smoothly with her white Astral or Nivea hand cream, her hands lay there silently still yet showing her troubles, silky with a little hint of white from the luscious thick lashings of cream on them and shiny oily skin oozing even more with the cream.

As I take a deep breath in, I can sense her Coco Chanel scent all around the room almost as if it's not in the air but within us and yet its masked like the morning dew, wet and damp and yet calming and then I breath out, it lessens. I smile as I have this strange sense of life in here but why do I think about life? There are two people now in this room one who is inquisitive and the other who is no longer. Gently I start talking to her but there was no response so without even fluttering an eyelid or itching or scratching those naughty bits. I could hear myself talking at her which she always hated and I did so often because at times it was the only way of getting her to actually listen with her full undivided attention.

As for her, she either didn't speak which was quite noticeable and yet people said she wasn't much of a talker and yet I have heard her talk beyond belief, especially with father but she always spoke whilst looking at the person who she was talking to or listening to, proper eye to eye contact but where there should have been that proper contact, there just wasn't. She would look at papa and speak to him not at him and never raised her tone to him but he always did, his words reflected his tone as she remained quite monotonous and his eye contact would hither and thither all over the place, unlike her. She would focus on him whilst speaking, reading into his words and looking deep into his lips and then she would quietly look at the empty things in an instance, at the watered down colours of the walls or the feet mark on the cold tiled floor or at the bright purple dusky passion fruit which had no passion in it any longer as it had been a permanent fixture in the fruit bowl for a while. She looked as empty and still as all these things that she looked at. When father didn't look 'at you' but spoke to you it meant that he was angry so really we both knew where we were with him, unlike her. When she spoke those empty words I could imagine her standing by the river that had no bed, so deep and yet so volatile and self-destructive and yet a river maybe, with no water.

"Ma, what's the matter, why aren't you getting up, let's look out of the window together." There's a lot of election fever outside and Papa's gone and I don't think he will be back till really late that is till he finds out if he's won which will be in the wee hours of the morning. If he's won like last time then he will be out celebrating with his mates and then he will be expecting you to help with the lunch treat for all of them as we look on and feel the jealousy whilst watching them enjoying themselves whilst we both serenade and listen and peer through the crack of the door whilst observing their ill-mannered habits of laughing out of control, loud gestures, rude remarks of people and eating and drinking themselves to madness. Mind you, as we always say we cannot complain because we do get our turn in the evening when it's just us three in a classy restaurant where father hates the music but you love, where violins and classical and old time classics get played live for you but he couldn't care less about them and food that's given in dribs and drabs the way you like it but he cannot eat that slowly but then, that evening is all about you, so that's good. He'll thank you for always supporting him and you then think that maybe, just maybe all will be good now and then I see that empty thing in your eyes when it's time to leave?'

I kneel beside her face, its warm sweet and tender and vulnerably young and even though she's only thirty six the smiling lines around her eyes and the stress lines on her forehead show that she is every bit a married woman. Her white pearl smile against her damson lips which are covered carefully by the red lipstick perfectly matching her veil now masking nearly half of her face. Her complexion was always the same since I can remember, dark and dusky, never tanned like fathers, or pale or even olive like mine. Her eyes dark, desirable and destined to be found but she was never in search of anything herself except for the one thing so precious, time, time that she could spend with just him and her and I think that that time was only when they went to bed and even then, she would often go by herself, watching out of the window waiting for him.

He would be downstairs with his mates, playing cards, chess, draughts and many other games and at times just sitting, smoking and drinking with them. He never ever drank himself silly as I have never smelt it from him or seen him drunk but I knew when he had some as his laughter was louder than his normal. I have never seen mother with her friends socializing ever but she says that she does that only when father and I are both out and she never went out with them in the evenings leaving us at home alone.

Even now as she lies here, there is that silent and still look in her face and as my nose nears her sweet breath, its heat has lost its spark, her breath was no longer as warm almost as if she's caught the chill of death but then how could she. Its mid-May, the summer is still serenading in glory. She doesn't utter a word, but nods ever so slightly like a shy lifeless butterfly, her nod that is a symbol of her wanting me to come even closer to her and now I sit on the floor and my face is real close to hers. I can see her baby fine black nostril hair but, they are embedded so tightly inside her round perfectly small nose and then her nostril closes tight and she turns her head and seals my right cheek with her wet glossy lips, a perfect pucker, it hasn't spoilt her lipstick, it's still perfect, like her, not tainted, not stained but too deep to reach.

I smile widely as this pleases me a lot and I start talking by telling her that she needs to get up and we can go down and watch television as her favourite Indian dramas are on as they always are, all day long. She loved them as they symbolized the life of an Indian woman, just like her. Her eyes became somewhat glazed not focused and for the first time ever her pupils seem to be getting bigger but I know I am imagining it, but I definitely don't imagine the tear that has just streaked out from her right eye and as I wipe away the smile from my face, I quickly put my hand under the corner of her eye and catch her tear drop. A slow drip drip and I wait for the tear from the left eye to dribble over the nose and down the right cheek but the liquid has evaporated on her not so warm skin and even though her face is wet, no tear drop falls on my hand. "Ma, why are you crying?" I don't know how many times I repeated this but like a person who is totally unaware of their own existence, she doesn't hear or reply. I was waiting for her to console me, to kiss me again, to take away the pain inside of me now. I wanted her to ease the aching in my throat but above all, I wanted her to catch my tears as she has done so many times, not that I cry often and nor does she, but she did today and I did what she does. She always said tears were priceless and should never be wasted, she would catch them and let them dry on her hand or she would rub them on her head.

I sit and sit and sit again and I know that a few hours have passed and Papa is not back and no one else is at home. I know I have to keep her red veil on her head for her as she has lost her own dignity and I make sure that mine is on as well, it is and hers is as well. I have sat here crying in silence, I have sat here crying in agony and pain that is too deep to explain but I know it's all in vain. The golden silent moments are not peaceful at the moment only silent, the movements have stretched themselves out just like the way she's stretched out, she is at peace, her arms still dangling now lifelessly and as I look closely from the corner of my eye, her fingers look like the shade of red and purple and yet they don't look hot. I look closely at her eyes and I know that she's staring but I cannot be worried because she is with me and within me, so deep, it would be impossible to separate us into two individuals.

I stare back at her almost blindly. I can see her but without actually staring at her but I don't like her look so I gently put my left hand over her left eye and then over her right but her glare is exactly the same. My hand trembles but I find the strength to slide her eyelid shut one by one, she does nothing to stop me and I try to close her big teethed quivered mouth but it doesn't close, so instead I smell her still breath. I close my eyes and imagine her with her eyes open, quickly I open my eyes. She's still asleep or something like that. She's silent but I am silently crying, she's peaceful but I am not. I am alive but I don't want to think about the rest! A beautiful lady, a mother and wife dignified in her red veil still covering her - that was her life.

Chapter 2

I move away from Ma but even though my mind has, my feet slither almost as if they are unable to lift themselves off from the heavy cloned floor and away from her heavy body and yet she's not heavy. The slow quivering of my own body has not meant that my soul has left her; no I am very much with her, so I quickly sit on the day bed right in front of the window. It is still light outside and it doesn't go dark till around half eight so I still have time to visualize the activity of the outside. I have a while yet and there's a strange tingling sensation within my body an unrest kind of shiver working its way down my spine. If only Papa came home early today but alas that is impossible as people are in full swing of the voting mania and then, he will still await for his eagerly awaited joy of having power not only of us, and his household but of all these idiots outside and yet these slum kids who sit outside every day, no one can control them ever.

Identical idiots who don't even know why they are voting, who they are voting for and what it means for them but, they still want to have that small bit of power and yet they will all be disappointed and so are we both today. I don't need glasses to see outside, in fact none of us in this house wear spectacles but, why can't these people see what they are being dominated by, they will not even know that in many countries it's called democracy but it doesn't work like that here.

It's not fair out there or in here. Then men are all in similar clothes, some with long tops, over flowing long skirts, rubber or plastic and faded flip flop well-worn at the side of the inner sole which resemble their clothes. Faded colours, worn and tired brown chests gathered and shiny with the suns heat, greasy smeared faces and black hair smothered all smooth except the excessive amount of tired sun damaged faces and necks full of wrinkles. Nothing can smooth them.

Lakeed, the little girl no more than about eight years of age, sits quiet near our bungalow as normal and she is quite unaware as to the fact that she is busily scratching the paint off the next door neighbour's gate with her silently polished silver key; maybe she should put it into her undergarments before she gets a clip around her ear holes, it will knock sense into her but then she wouldn't be put off by that as she is properly used to it by now. That's how the vulnerable get treated regularly, so what's new?

The next door neighbour's young daughter Bippy, not married yet but ready for it, hips swaying, shoulders uptight and boobs half open to the world to see, slowly comes out and quietly goes to the little scratchy girl. "You little tramp, here's a drink carton for you, have it and then clear off and yes listen, go and have a wash stink bomb and stop scratching your head, go and clear your nits elsewhere." There's no remorse in her action or tone as she throws the drink at her. The little girl gently utters "My name's not stink bomb, it's

Lucky." The big girl shakes her head and turns her back to Lakeed whilst rubbishing her in the usual way, saying "Lucky, why of course Lakeed you are."

Big bungalows, big families, big money and lack of big hearts, that's all of us after all I have never offered the outside people a drink ever. They are the generation of beggars and we the generation of givers and yet I have never given anyone anything yet, nor have I seen Mother do so either. That was Father's job and he did it without even thinking, whenever he left home, whoever was outside our house he would always give them something, mostly money and on many occasions he would go and give them flour from our pantry so they could go home and mothers could bake bread or fruit to eat and I have often seen Kaka also giving, but he always had a naughty yet funnily enough a nice way of giving.

Many times on our journey to school or back home he would often put his hand out of the car and give them beggars who he called "dirty creatures from the dirty drain" some snacks which he always had with him. Some of his delights were almonds, raisins and of course traditional Indian fried snacks such as samosas and pakoras, these were always delicious. He would never give the delights to the beggars but always threw the food at them, not to them and the beggars like kids to candy would quickly try to gather his gifts for themselves and all the while looking at him whilst saying "Thank you sir, thank you kind sir," with their wide smile so warm and genuine and most of them with a teeth missing and tobacco stains and yet their hearts filled with joy. Dark unhealthy little boys with their runny noses wiped across their cheeks and little girls with hungry looks and long straight plaits but somehow we noticed and yet all these things didn't really matter so long as they all had a little bit to eat.

That was happiness even though Kaka always tried to slap them on the back of the head or around the cheek wherever he could reach and if anyone dared to reply back he would always shout "Why don't you crawl back to the gutter where you belong." It didn't bother them, or so it seemed. That was nasty and my own impression of Kaka was nasty too because every time he said this, my head always painted a picture of him as being one of them and not us. He acted as if he was one of us yet far more superior than they were. He was in a way because he had a shirt of his back that had no holes in it and his trousers were the iron free ones so always looked good and he always got his shoes polished everyday by the shoe shine boy outside my school, on the street and furthermore, he had a bungalow to live in, yes he lived in his own quarters in our bungalow. His bread was buttered on both sides.

"Well, Ma, let me start by telling you what's happening outside." Slowly I wipe away the dust that caught my eye not deliberately of course. I can feel the slow pain in my eye but this is not what has made tears spill from it. The warm tears speedily drip from the centre and into my lap, I place my hands on my lap to catch them and without even thinking about my actions, I rub my damp palms over my veil. It's still secured tightly enough and I stare back at Ma to make sure her veil is also on. It is, that's good. She's so peaceful but there's so much turbulence within me.

I sit and I don't know what to do so instead I sit and cry, that is the only thing that has come naturally right now. I don't know how I managed to cry silently and talk loudly but I did and relentless to say I told her all about the day at school and the songs that Kaka played in the car and that Papa left straight away and there's been no sign of any jubilation just yet and the votes have not been counted yet but the crowds are still going from sane direction to the silly direction, whilst the dismal almost straight lamppost guides them to their desired direction and the old woman who forever wears her thick, almost double glazed glasses so she too can see her own life's direction and yet she stands with her grey sari on and her white flip flops and brittle uncut dirty toenails within her flip flops. There's no grace, but who is grace? She stands with her legs wide apart her hands on her waist and with a kind smile, she squints her nose as it helps her glasses stay up on the rock of her nose. Her bare and hollow chocolate face shows her front missing teeth as she pushes her top jaw sweetly into the lower one, it rests peacefully just like her. What does she do here anyway?

She comes every day and she is very full of life and yet she decides to stand there very still without a veil on and then there is my mother who is still veiled and she decides not to move and did have a choice but the old woman maybe doesn't have any real choices. I wonder if should give her a name? Yes, it's not nice to keep calling her little lady. Little Margaret Thatcher, that's what she looked like, so I think I'll call her Maggie.

I have pressed my nose against this big window whilst observing Maggie and now with the warm heat of my own body, it's steamed up nicely but then no one can see in anyway. My nose feels cold and I feel isolated, I can feel the goose pimples on my arms, it was warm outside and in here as well and yet I was feeling cold, it seemed frightening. She looked like how I felt right now. I move away from the window as I don't really want to see the life, yes a life outside.

I kneel right beside my mother as she lays peacefully still and I sit on my legs with my knees bent, I cannot feel her breath or her heat and maybe she is feeling cold just like me but even though I remain sitting comfortably, I don't feel that comforted from my heart within. My trembling hands touch her forehead as I straighten her frown lines but they remain as before, maybe it's because her forehead is not warm anymore. I can keep her soul warm until father comes back whenever that will be. I don't want to leave her now but I feel helpless and don't really know quite what to do, after all, all the decisions are normally

36

made by the adults and I just obey. I feel uneasy so I quickly try and press mothers veil to the side of her face, yes that position hasn't changed but I just wanted to make sure.

I then move my wide hips off from the floor and from the corner of my right eye I feel that I saw blood however I really don't have the time or the inclination to think of it right now and its almost as if the bloods just rung a big red bell in my ears. I sit and focus and realise that it's the dull ringing of the house telephone, yes that's right it's a red telephone ringing. I haven't got the time to answer that call as I am far too busy. I go over to the big dresser mirror and look at myself from the top to bottom. In front of me stands a woman's body and yet I don't feel like one. I hold the veil firmly down, yes it does age me but then it gives me honour, dignity and respect, that's what Ma always said, that is exactly the words she used to use.

In the last hour and a half I have taken out Ma's scarves and one by one I have put them on my head and peeled them down like glue, every one of those colours tells a different story. The red one will be for the time that I get married, when I have to grow up and become an adult, the orange for the week leading up to my wedding, all the trials and intricacy of the henna colours, the yellow for the haldi that will be pasted to give a glowing colour and the green for when I go on my honey moon to the place where the grass in always green wherever that may be and the blue simply because the sun is always shining well at least most of the time in India and it is here that I will wed. That is what my life will be as an adult but I do have years yet as I am only sixteen, a school kid yet. That was what Ma's life was and I am going to wear her veils and her shoes one day. My heart murmurs away.

"Get up child, get up child." I could hear the soft murmurs of these words ringing in my ears but I thought I was dreaming but indeed I was not. Papa was standing in front of me with a dead look in his eyes and motionless. "Did you win Papa?" he looked down "Win, no darling we have all lost, you and I have lost your Ma and she, our beautiful love has lost her life and Mimi it's all my fault, dearest Meera its all my fault." I get up from my lying position on the floor and with all the colours of the rainbow all around me I feel a bit puzzled, when did I actually dose off on the floor and what time could it be now and when did Papa come home and what has happened in between the time whilst I was soundly asleep and almost dead to the world. Acting almost like a mature young lady I explained how Ma was not and couldn't be dead. She could only be asleep and so pleaded with him to let her remain peaceful. With great disappointment in his words he uttered that she was now peaceful forever.

I looked at the swinging seat, it was peacefully moving as time does but Ma was no longer on there and as I stood there looking at it, all I could remember was the fact that not that long ago she laid there. I could still smell her, her tainted body smell lingering amongst the sweet almond musky smell from her perfume. I ran and took her position and sat exactly where she had laid, Papa came and joined me, we both reached out for one another and hugged and it felt as if all my pains had been warmed away. I felt comforted by someone whose own heart and pulse were beating faster than mine, so very much alive. I could feel his beating heart on top of that laid his hairy chest as it pressed tightly against me. We often hugged each other but never this tight, it felt ever go good as I sobbed as he wiped away my tears and then he cried and I wiped his wet eyes with my veil still snoozed around my neck and head.

We both got up from the swinging chair and Papa led me into the big sitting room downstairs where only guests sat but this room now looked so different. The room full of all white leather furniture had been serenaded into one corner and a big white clinical sheet rough and yet crease free covered the furniture and the big television. The floor was covered with rugs and a covering of a white sheet. Everything was white including what my Ma was covered in and now laying on the floor there was a dark dusky woman lying underneath a white sheet on a white rug. Her head was covered with a colourful veil and I could still see her long luscious black hair. I can also see from the corners of my eye the black chandeliers beaming in full light and the black pearled not so dead lamps in the two corners near the door. They outstretched the light and radiate the room. The room was empty except for Mother, Father, Kaka and me. In fact, so was the remainder of this big house, empty.

I took my seat next to Ma, her dark hair just like darkness outside of the window and yet it looked very white and bright in here. Her dark lashes covering her dark pupils closed to the world and as I closed my own eyes all I see is darkness, not just in my eyes but deep down inside I don't know exactly where. The big deep black hole is too far for me to reach almost so deep that it felt as if it was slowly swallowing me within it. I scream and father silently sobs, my loud bellowing cries reach loudly around the house and yet no one listens or replies. I can hear some faint crying and as I look behind me its Kaka, gracefully he's crying with a handkerchief on his mouth whilst facing the wall like a naughty child full of embarrassment but at this moment he's neither of those.

My eyelids feel so heavy even though I know that I have slept but because of the crying they feel sore and heavy and I can feel the puffiness of the top lids. Father stands beside me and his hand on his eyes and the pain in his heart and yet, with all the will in the world in trying to comfort me, it's a shame he couldn't do that for her. I sit with my head in my hands and I feel the tears running onto my palms and down the arms and even though I don't look up or around me, I can sense lots of brown clean feet treading their ways into this white room and their white flowing suits and saris all perfectly crisp and clean neatly tapered around them as the torsos quietly sit on their bottoms and utter their sorrowful prayers. I'm inquisitive to know who has come and yet I am just too tired to lift my head.

The room seems to be going round and round or is it my head that is so full of the mad circles or is it, the fact that I am just too tired to know but whatever it is, I'm almost quite numb to the whole environment. More and more feet slowly whisper their way in and I can hear the feet slowly shuffling off the flip flops just outside the room and my mother lays in the centre but near the back of the room beside the big chunky white window and I am near her and yet unaware of the others and then, it's almost as if life has just re awoken and I have remembered that the bright sun has slowly started to rise from nowhere and seep through the window, the dust in the air filters down.

I open my eyes but they felt as if they were not even open but through the creeks of the dim light that was creeping through, I could smell the room. I can smell the room being nearly full. All of the sudden I look up and look around and sense the bigness of this room and the white muffled faces in front of the dark faces mingling with the "well to do" faces all paraded and seated in a civilised obedient manner, perfectly criss-cross legs and arms with clean nails and no dirt stuck in between and proper while veils on the females heads and men with the white handkerchiefs covering their heads.

The women all seated on the left, and the men

41

all on the right. A real segregation of sexes, no one is looking at anyone as they all look down on grief, long faces, narrowed eyes and wide straight mouths and as my site looks further on I can see the peoples of the street lining just inside of this big room. The big white-clothed woman who always stands outside our house around four o' clock in the afternoon whom they call Tara and Maggie is here with her legs wide open and her hands on her waist as ever. She is first in the queue and now she sits like everyone else. She squats on her backside with her feet firmly on the ground and her arms now braced around her legs as she rubs her hands together with a firm "tut tut" in a pity, outraged to the sad news. You can hear her hands rubbing together like fine sandpaper and yet she is perfectly calm and comfortable. None of these people here are actually grieving but they are here to pay their respects and the ones just outside this room are all here just to have a good feed as it is customary for them to turn up on all occasions of death, birth and marriages and no one turns them out of their homes.

I don't know what to do or how I should behave but Mother always told me a daughter needs to be dignified at deaths and marriages and that a woman must know exactly what to do on occasions, otherwise a mother has not taught the child well. That word dignified is going through my head, I don't know its real meaning and it sounds a bit of a difficult word to pronounce or to know the meaning of it, so how would I know how to be dignified. I could look it up but can't ask these people its meaning, I have a computer and the internet but I think life will teach me what that word means as for now, if I act exactly the way all these people are, then that will be perfectly dignified. I slowly slide my legs out from underneath me and sit on my backside and then elegantly trying without succeeding I try to criss-cross my legs in a perfect shape. There is a gap between my knees and their knees, their feet are twined together more and their knees are level to their hips but mine are parched out in a yoga position and I know that's not dignified and so slowly I correct that position. It hurts but I can bare this pain unlike the one inside.

I take my veil ends and firmly wrap them tightly around my neck it feels as if mother is hugging my slim long neck, suffocating but it keeps me tightly focused and without making much of a noise, I shuffle my feet further into my body and push my knees inwards with firm pressure from my hands. I measure the straight line from my hands from the hip to the knee. It's parallel now, that's dignified. I sit like a mother but look like a mummy wrapped up tight. Taking a deep breath in I cannot smell my mother anymore but I can sense all of these people in front of me. I stare at all of them one by one, they all look the same, almost like my mother except that she is lying down and they are sitting upright and uptight, everyone is in white except for me. A big tall man comes into the room and all of a sudden everyone looks up at him, he looks like one of them. I keep an eye on him as he quickly walks to the front row and parches his big bulky body on the floor, he raised his brow and looked un-unnervingly into my eyes. It's Father, he has taken his colourful clothes off.

It is strange how my heart and soul didn't want to except the fact that mother was absolutely dead now so there was no chance of her waking up and the sheer fact that father's dressed in his funeral white, suddenly it all became quite real. He whispered something to the man sitting behind him who whispered to the one next to him and so one until the one on the end of the first row whispered to the lady who sat at the end of the ladies row. Slowly she gracefully got up pulled her dress firmly down against her legs and gazing all the while onto the floor and quietly comes over to where I sat. I chose to ignore her even though I knew that she started to say something but I acted ignorant and all the while, I was just staring at Mother's face.

I looked peacefully and calmly at mothers face but she didn't stare back and I could still see the almost black feel of the woman dressed in white soldering herself over me. She calmly pushed her feet under my knees and gently gave me a quick shove; it was a sign for me to get up. I don't like to be told or pushed around so I moved over a little, ignored her and gently started to stroke mother instead. I could hear a gentle voice of a mother soothingly telling me to get up and get changed into something appropriate but why should I listen as it wasn't my own mother telling me and I don't have to listen to them, why should I? Why the hell do I have to change my clothes? I don't have to follow their rules. I don't want to be just like them.

I sat staring into mothers aged skin, the pores of the skin so visible on the chin with the strong light I can see the rippled cracks of her foundation laying on top of the tiny baby hair on the face. Somehow she looks fragile and delicate and even though its unexplainable I needed to look at her with more attention to notice things clearly and I remember all the times that the beautician used to come to do things that I had no knowledge of because, I was not allowed to watch but was promised that once I finished school and after college, I would be allowed to get my eyebrows done but only if I was going to go to university. All those decisions but now no one can carry them out. I look closely at her eyebrows, thick, black and plentiful and perfectly manicured into a gentle shape, almost natural. She could have been almost dead but not really if only father had come home on time but then he never does and what is "on time."

I see her eyebrows and think of my own and I want mine to be a replica of hers and so with both of my hands I stroke my own into the same shape as hers. Maybe if I carry on they will be the same shape. My tears have started to flow again as I know I have missed the chance of getting my

45

eyebrows threaded and the more that I cry the faster my strokes get. I carry on and even though by now, the ladies standing next to me have both attempted to pick me up from either side and start to drag me along the middle of the room all the way to the end nearing the big door and then straight through the doorway where Tara and Maggie stood. My legs have felt the cold tiled floor and then suddenly I get up and stand next to Maggie. I look into her empty eyes and then I look down at her wide legs as she looks on with her almost magnifying spectacles, she squints a little and tries really hard to peer into my eyes closely. I feel like swearing at her because I don't want her to pity me and I imitate her by standing with my legs wide apart just like her, she shakes her head and runs her sand like hands together "Oh God, Oh God, poor child, tut, tut."

I was calm and still before her words 'poor child' and now these two words kept ringing in my ears like the bells ringing on the top of any hour but these bells wouldn't stop and I wanted them to stop but they wouldn't so I started to shout louder than the noise of the bell "I am not poor, I am rich, look I live in this bungalow with father and mother, I am not poor do you hear me Tara and Maggie." I don't know how many times I repeated this but I know I said it till the words could no longer come out and the only thing that anyone could hear was, my crying. The outside people all cluttered in the hallway stared, their faces with empty looks, their hollow cheeks dimpled against their chalky flesh, small thin bony noses with hardly any flesh on them and eyes that have never seen make up and yet without uttering a word, they told so many stories. Why did they all have to come here and why are they looking at me?

I have to be dignified, I stand up straight tall and make sure that both of my feet are touching together and those big chunky women can lead me up the stairs, and then they show me their finger so that I could lead them to my bedroom. Out of the ten bedrooms, mine had the biggest door and slowly we all three go inside and I sit lazily on my bed. This bed has not been slept in, the sheet in still crisp and clear and there is a tiny ripple where my back lays. The duvet and blanket are pushed to the end. End of someone's life, end of a mother's journey, end of a child's mother and the end of wearing colourful clothes. "She's a stubborn mule" whispered one of the women as she busily rummaged through my clothes and as the other woman looked at me from the corner of the right eye, she bit her lip as to acknowledge the fact that I had heard. I stared at her as she tried hard not to stare at me, quietly I replied "I am not a mule, in fact your face is exactly like a mule's, so now what?" She quietly utters a dull cough from her ever so dry throat almost as if someone was shouting into a dry and empty well.

Both look like proper maids, gently moving one hanger along to look at the next one, all in search of that white suit or sari. All the hangers in my wardrobe are wooden, exactly the same but they all hold different parts of my life. Slowly these mules have taken out about six different hangers with white clothes hanging on them, the nice lady who doesn't really look at me, one by one she holds up the hangers for me to see and one by one I reject them all and then, she moves her chest up and down as she sighs and takes a deep breath in and then with a big sigh again, she blows out the air through her nose, her nostrils open up a little and then she's calm. They both stand in front of me with their hands on their hips waiting for what? "Get changed and then come down, all in white please." said the stern looking woman who thought I was the mule. I looked closely at her face and then I snapped by telling her to take her donkey face and get lost and not tell me what to do, with that they both raised their eyebrows in utter disgust and go towards the door. "Get lost mules. Piss of donkeys, and bye bye." I showed no remorse and I don't even look at them but I do slam the heavy door on their backs "ee oo ee oo." The noise of the mule stops but the crying persists louder than ever and really, I don't know what I am doing here and how I got here today. I lay on my bed looking at the red ceiling. It's so warm and colourful yet I feel empty and forlorn. It's almost as if I had been standing on a big red carpet and now it's been pulled out from under my feel, gutted with everything lost in between.

My head in spinning and all around me I can see and visualise my life with mother and I capture it all in one simple word "joy" and then I pick up my small hand held mirror and look at the joy it's not there anymore, the mirror never lies. I don't know how slowly or quickly time has passed by but I can smell food. The distinctive smell of sweet semolina and the hot fluffy and flat oily bread that was call puri and stuffed parathas and peshawari naan. The strong aroma craves within me to get up and eat or at least wake up and go downstairs for food after all, it is breakfast time and that means it must have been about seven o'clock now. I am still in my colourful clothes like an obedient child of sixteen, I pick up the first white suit that I can see and put it on. It does have a white scarf with it and against my jet black hair it looks quite nice, colours of death and dignity. I have to punish myself and I need to be punished after all that is what God is doing to me now, after all, I did not get to her in time and I didn't know what to do so I need to be punished.

I wrap the scarf tightly around my neck like a tight snooze but even this won't take me to the place she is. I slowly take myself out of my room and before I shut the heavy door behind me, I look at it again, what a mess those stupid donkeys have made, they've left all the clothes on the edge of my bed. I have left them there as well which means all of these are now dirty after all I don't wear my clothes more than once and then I throw my clothes on the floor and mother always picks them up, washes, irons and hangs them back into my wardrobe.

Barefooted and bare skinned I make my way

49

down the big stairway slowly one by one I climb down each hurdled step whilst counting it 39, 40. The smell is arousing in the dining room and the curls of the smoked aroma smother me and I quietly go and stand outside the dining room. The chattering of the mouths of the outside people as they busily tuck into the feast laid out for them, a full desi Indian style breakfast with chickpeas and a whole feast of rusks and breads with boiled eggs served in trays and flasks of hot tea with cardamom and cinnamon smells streaming out. Kaka is standing in the corner asking if anyone needs anything else and politely telling everyone to eat to their hearts' desire, after all, no one can die with the dead, so he says. No one's listening to his commentary now as men and women mingle their words with one another and eat with their unwashed hands and at this moment in time so am I and as I look on, no one looks at me because they are all looking into their plates. Their mouths not even half-empty but their hand is already full of food morsels ready and waiting.

When they have had enough, they burp, wipe away the food remains on their sleeves and then sip the hot delicious tea and then start round two of food. Their waists so wafer thin with their bewithered bodies, their crackly bones seeping through their tops and I wonder how they can eat so much. How can there be so much space in their flat stomachs its strange, but before they were all quiet and still but now they are all loud and moving and yet, they are still sitting in the house of the dead. The woman with the course hands sits near the door and shows me her finger as to say that I "can" sit next to her to eat. I look away and slowly the serving staff walk past me to serve more food to them. Bowls of homemade yogurt, luscious thick whole milk and trays of firm juicy red rosy apples and tender yet firm slightly tainted bananas. I stand and watch and just as I have contemplated, as soon as the trays are put on the floor the yogurt is tucked into with bare hands, the remainders of the liquid running down the fingers and the corners of the dark mouths and the fruits quickly get slipped into either their laps, pockets or the spare hand. Why did it take my mother to die and leave us for these outside people to get properly fed?

I enter the visitors' room again where my mother is still waiting for me and I go and sit beside her. Men and women chanting some hysterical and delirious prayers and there is a fat man suiting in one corner leading the prayer procession. Kaka comes in with a very polite face and tells everyone that they must have breakfast as its being served for them all, some resist and others go straight away and a few are prompted but the big airy room is now clear of people except for the fat man who looks almost like a bouncer. He carries on with his recitations of which I understand very little of and father and I look at one another. Father takes his right hand and outs it to his mouth as to tell me to go and eat. I shake my head. He calls Kaka which is a word for a male child and he tells him to bring food in for me but I keep insisting that I am not eating.

Kaka brings the food anyway, two trays of a variety of breakfast and puts it by my side quietly. I slide it away from me even though my tiny tummy is yearning for it. My heart is yearning for the woman who is laying in front of me and the forbidden milk that I can smell but don't remember and somewhere within my sole, my senses can smell her almost as if she smells like a new born baby and no more of her Chanel perfume, even though I can still smell the food close to me I raise my right hand and take a deep breath in and now I can really smell that breast milk. I have been staring at her face for so long now and it seems as if it's been hours and hours and then a group of six women come in and a small bed in carted in by four strong men and gently the women pick mother up and place her on the bed that is cradled on the floor. The men butch and macho with bushy moustaches take the burden of the bed, cold pine frames with thick tight strapping covered with mother and the white sheet on top, her colourful clothes on top of her weight and her soul, she rides along in silence.

The men carry her along as if she is on her final leg of her journey but even I know that she still has a final farewell journey yet and suddenly it has clicked in my tiny head that she is being taken for preparations before her final farewell. The cleansing ritual of the body from the outside and the spiritual cleaning from within is going to take place and I know that it's the duty of relatives to do this but there is no other family member here. I look up at Father and he has this look of helplessness his facial expressions so still and his eyes just looking at me and as I look around the room, all the outside people seem to have vanished from the dining area away from the entrance of this big room they are all outside now. At least they are happy now. I wonder if father is in a way happy because I can still hear the election fever and he must be feeling it deep down inside, has he won or not.

The respected guests have all moved around into a circle and waiters all dressed in black and white come in one by one and place a variety of breakfast foods, hot tea, napkins, sparkling silver dessert spoons and perfectly clean dinner plates surround the trays of food. The not so hungry mouths stay closed and their eyes peer on the rustic lines of the dining room floor. The smells of the hot food make my mouth feel alive once again and from all the food I can smell the turnip, potato and radish stuffed parathas. Mother always made these and she always said that these were a good start to the day. We had parathas for breakfast and a composition of spicy chickpeas and greasy flatbreads with sweet pastries and hot semolina pudding made from clarified ghee. Food fit for thoroughbreds here in India. Butter from natural sources, the milking of organic cows in the backyard, the churning of the milk in the bucket and the forming of pure full fat cream is what our diets are all about. Smell of home. Kaka is looking straight at me whilst standing at the door and there is a repetition of his words "Please let me know if you need anything else." No one takes the slightest bit of notice and no one is interested in eating much unlike the people from the outside.

I run and quickly take a paratha, I roll it up and for a while I stand there smelling it, it smells like her first thing in the morning as that was the only time she made food and was surrounded by the smells. No wonder she always took a shower after breakfast and she never cleaned or washed after breakfast as Tara always came after dropping her children off to school and she attended to the kitchen and cleaned the house. She cooked lunch, cleaned up again and then got dinner ready and laid it out on the table and then she would leave. At times Mother washed up in the evenings, occasionally I would do it but father never did so as he always said that was a woman's chore and often dishes would be piled in the sink for the next day duties.

The food rests so snugly within my fist and the aroma stays strong and I run behind all of those people who are leaving now. Mother is the highest of them all but whilst they carry her she utters no words. She is carried out to the back courtyard and then into the big room at the back of the bungalow where the spare things were stored. She was not anything spare or unneeded like the rifles, guns, duvets still packed in their plastics, drink bottles and cans of food like KP peanuts and roasted cashew nuts. The storage room was not going to store her because she was going to be stored in the ground. She wasn't spare but she was spared from our lives. Slowly the doors opened wide and the lights beam in full, no one utters a word and there is great silence. Kaka follows me with his head down in grief.

There are wooden pallets that are stacked up and the slatted bed is placed in position and mother lays and I take her hand and my other hand is still fisted full of food. I can still smell the food in my hand. It's still warm and delicious and yet I have not tasted it today. The women start to fumble around just the way mother used to in her wardrobe and I stand beside them. No one is looking at me except for Kaka. The other men have all left and slowly I raise my right hand and I take the food close to mothers nose, she's not interested and nor am I. slowly both of my hands rest by my hips now as the tears rest neatly like slow streams down my face. I start to kiss her forehead, it should have been exactly the way it was when I kissed her yesterday but it wasn't, it was cold, lifeless and still dusky. There was no smell of motherly milk anymore and I could smell her skin, my lips could feel her baby hair but she didn't kiss me in return. My pain throttled in my throat but hers seemed so still. Had the mother left this woman?

Chapter 3

Family members are supposed to wash the person who cannot wash themselves, not hospitals and not outsiders or neighbours but it is local people here and they have not been told to do any of this and yet they are organising what our family and I are supposed to do. I know the female family members always wash the female and vice versa then get them ready in their "almost" wedding clothes, their best clothes and their best veil are all worn and their hair combed and face made up as if they are still alive and then they get put onto the strappy bed once more and finally all the female members who did wash the person have to go and wash themselves and change into clean clothes, ready to rid yourselves of that person and any memory that you may have of them. I don't want that to happen so I make sure that I don't take my eyes off her for even a second. I keep a firm look on her through my watery glazed eyes and I can hear my stomach rumbling and I start to wonder in my head whether Mama's stomach is rumbling as well? Why wouldn't it be, she is a human after all?

I show Mama the food in my hand, she doesn't seem so happy to see it and I cannot eat yet because the tears won't let any food down the throat, there seems to be a big bump of liquid dying to get out and slowly but surely it is being released through my eyes. She doesn't say a thing; she doesn't look at me or even respond to the food that I am offering her. I don't want the mules to hear so I keep repeating the same words quietly to mother, she can hear me and they can't. "Mama, have some food please Mama, for my sake, have some, please, please...." I think she cannot understand what I am saying because I am speaking quietly and she is asleep, so lost in her sleep, but soon she will find her way back to me.

I can hear flutters in my eardrum the fly busily playing away, the mosquito's making a nuisance of themselves with their constant roaming everywhere and on everyone and the queen bee along with a few wasps accompanying her all gather in this storage room to see what is being stored today and as they all buzz and hiss for their prey, I wish that they were all lying here instead of mother. They come and pester her by playing on her face and I can feel the anger get excited inside of me. I raise my left hand and start to fan mothers face and soon, they find someone else to amuse themselves with. A few of them sit on my right hand as they too can smell the food closely clasped in my fist. They want a morsel of it but it's for Mother, not them. Why can't she smell it and now it's as if I can't smell it either.

"Put the electric fan on Ranif, there's a plug in that corner and the switch is on the right, it will keep these pests away," urged the leader of this pack, slithering their way into our business.

"Yes, good idea Koyna" and quietly she goes and does what she was told. The pests have left our small area as they desperately go and search of someone else. The hosepipe in the corner in turned on and a yellow pale bucket with no special purpose in life waits for the water to spill into her and I stand and wonder how cold and cooling the water must be. If it's from the well, it's cool but if it's from the water pipe it's probably not. The pink sunlight soap comes out of its protective wrapper and like a military man it awaits to go into action. There are two clean blue towels carefully folded awaiting and then the leader of the pack starts to explain to me that mother was going to be undressed and then her hair and body would get washed and rinsed and dried and then I could choose her clothes and make up and they would put these on her and finally the men will come and put her on a clean bed and take her for cremation. Rather than listening to any of that, I choose to look and listen to mother instead!

The rules and the leader of the pack can say what they like I just continue to look at mother. "Mother please eat a little, please you eat and then I will eat as well, I am hungry." I take my closed fist and I look at it carefully even though I am not really looking at it at all even though my fist was smaller now and the food was oozing from the sides. I put it to mother's mouth and she doesn't take it or even open her mouth not even to utter a word. Silent tears are still flowing but I cannot hear myself cry but I can hear all these women talking slyly like hyena's chattering away and do they not know that mother can hear them even though I cannot. Mother doesn't eat and I don't want to, I stand alone without a way to turn to, I stand still, so very still. The women slowly push me to stand behind Mother's head so that they can get started and I observe.

Bit by bit they carefully caress the clothes away from her flesh and as they do so, I try to smell her but there is nothing that I can remind myself of the fact that this woman here was or is my mother, it's as if I'm looking at a piece of me but she has lost her voice and identity. For the first time ever I see her lying in full flesh, quickly I grab a blue towel, a man's towel and put it over this women's pride and dignity and yet she should not have a blue towel it is a man's towel and she has her own red towels and blue does not shade a woman's dignity. I think she has smiled but maybe I have missed it. The leader of the pack has gently uttered kind words of prayer whilst the others do their duty. She kindly tells me to stop crying as it is not good to do so whilst in the presence of the dead.

I quickly move my left hand and wipe away Mother's tears. The woman nods and whilst gently coming really close to me, she starts to say something to me but without even looking at me. I look away from Mother and look at her but her eyes watch the dripping water from Mother's shower. The clean soapy Radox aroma smells are just so comforting but they have not used Radox on her today. She then looks directly into my eyes and tells me to wipe "my tears" and not Mother's. I wipe away mothers tears again and somehow my own have now dried. There is an awkward kind of look on her face, the kind where you are trying to get through to someone and yet there is a brick wall that is in front of you and then you are trying hard to remain sensitive but its causing you so much frustration and the reason simply because you just don't know what to do.

"What is your name?" I ask her. She looks at me and there is a big slit going across her left cheek. I wonder what happened and how that got there. It is a cut not a scratch. "How did you get that cut on your cheek?" I ask, avoiding her gaze. Instead I look at her forehead. There are two big ditches at the beginning of her eyebrows at the top of the big hairs. She is stressed and worried and yes some people have these big ditches and are stressed and worried for nothing like her and then there are others like myself who have a whole life ahead of them to worry about! Which one of these situations is worse, a born worrier or having worries to worry about?

"My name in Mimi, well Papa and Ma both call me Mimi and Kaka does as well and that's most of my family really, but what use is a family if they all go away. Papa's family only visit on special occasions and most of them are abroad and as for Ma, well she had parents but they have decided to go to God instead of staying with her and she doesn't have siblings or relatives that I know of and you know what people are going to say about me. Oh yes, they are going to say that I don't have siblings either and I don't and they will be right to say so and I am talking gibberish now and I don't know why but it is better than not talking. I mean talking is better than not talking and talking is better than listening because to listen you have to focus on what's being said, the reality and the truth. But when you talk, you can say any crap that comes out without any thoughts really. I mean I talk out aloud all the time. Oh yes, you were telling me your name and why you have those worry lines and how you got your cut on the cheek?"

All the talk in the world couldn't take my eyes away from Ma and her forbidden beauty. She was as much a beauty now as she ever was. Her hair always coloured and never grey, her hands perfectly manicured never brittle or rough, her body skin soft and gentle, her feet soft without any dry coarse sandy paper feel and yet her life was like the latter. Her belly button so even and a perfect round small circle, you could slot a small round gem into it perfectly even though they say that when you have children your belly button gets stretched out of shape and I think it is true because she has only had me so it should be near perfect. Near perfect but she gave birth to me, so it shouldn't be perfect, did she actually give birth to me if so, how come she still looks perfect in every way? I quickly pull up my long top and look at my belly button. Mine is more perfect than hers, mine is small than hers. I put my tiny finger into it, it goes in well and then I put the same into Mother's belly button. There is some gap. That's poof that Mother's is bigger than mine, so hers is not perfect any more. That proves that she did give birth to me.

I cannot explain the look on these weird women's faces when I did that but then she's my mother and she's mine and I can do what I want, weirdos! "Didn't I ask you your name, it's not mule is it? You do have a name, right mule? Anyway there are lots of mules here today I think you know some mule called me a mule today."

"Look dear, no one is a mule, mules are animals we are all humans and I know you're upset and so you should be and I am sorry for your loss but it will get better after today, give yourself time dear," she uttered with dignity in a mellow and slow tone. I didn't hear all her words and I did smell her tobacco breath but it wasn't bad at all, it smelt strong, like a man's breath. Some peoples breath smells of tobacco because they smoke cigarettes but you're a woman, so why does yours smell, are you half a man? Ma never smoked but Papa did, so men smoke and women don't! "Listen dear, like I said," she tried patiently to explain.

"Don't dear me. I am not a deer or a reindeer or any sort of deer, so don't dear me, dear lady. I just asked you your name dear, that's all dear. What's the harm in telling me that, dear? I went on and on.

"I'm sorry, why don't you sit here on this chair and eat what you have in your hand?"

"No!" I shouted so loudly that they all stopped what they were doing and started staring at me. I continued with words that were going nowhere.

62

"This food is for Ma, she hasn't eaten since yesterday and I don't want to eat, it's for her!"

"Okay, but do you think you could go and get your favourite suit for your Ma and her make-up, something she can leave happily in."

With this I stopped looking at Ma and started looking at the cracks in between the bricks of this course wall, I am like one of these bricks! My eyes are dry, my nose sore, and my head aching with deep down pain. "My name is Sultana, Sultana, alright. Can you tell me if you are going to get the things or shall I ask Kaka?"

I look straight at her now and shout once again, "No."

She gently takes my left hand into hers and tries to console me, rubbing my hand and a bit of my arm as well as if I were aching there, but I wasn't, my pain was deep inside and then there was sultana offering me a consolation prize. That's how it is now so I quietly said "I will go and get them. Sultana, sultana's like raisins, sultana's, sultanas and raisins." She clicked her tongue as to signal that, that was a good idea but seemed a bit confused at the repetition. In complete utter silence I went straight back into the house, there were many faces looking here and looking there, the outside people were not inside, respected guests made this house their own but there seemed no signs of Papa nor Kaka. I wonder if they have gone to see if they have won the elections or not.

I quietly go upstairs almost as if I am a stranger in my own home now or is it not mine anymore and head for Ma's room. She must be lying on her swinging chair still. I go over to her but there is a stillness and cold emptiness in the air as if there are no words written in her diary that lies on her dressing table. The emptiness in here as if the hangers on her wardrobe have no clothes hanging on them anymore and as if the smell in the bedroom air has been put back into her room spray bottle. She sprays this every morning. This is the same room, same environment, but everything's really changed but what exactly?

Her clothes, lightly scented with her owns smells all line up eagerly awaiting for their next wear, I take off all of her suits and saris off the hangers, they dangle lopsided to and fro like the wet washing on the line, I throw all of the clothes onto the floor, it makes me feel helpless. What am I doing? I don't really know what I am doing but I know something for sure. Now that all the clothes are on the floor and I am lying on them, there is a comfortable and relaxing sensation within me as if she's wrapped me in her arms. That sensation is so soothing my lips are no longer dry as if the motherly thirst have been quenched , my eyes seem to be less dry and puffy and the aching in them has somewhat become a little more comfortable and cooling and the head that was beating with loud thumps has self-realized an inner calm and relaxation.

"Aren't you going to get up at all today, Meera? Let's both sit down with Kaka and talk at the table whilst we try to eat something. We will then sit

64

and chat like you used to with your Ma till bedtime and you know Meera, I don't know how much, if any sleep, I will be able to get but we both have to try. However, I am glad to see that you have had a good few hours of sleep, you needed it child." He talked I listened, he looked at me but I looked all around me, his clothes are still so fresh, clean and white but I was lying with my back on the many different colours of Ma's life. My right hand felt somewhat soggy and the fist had automatically opened but the food was still there, I clasp my fist.

"Don't move these clothes, Papa."

"No worries Meera," he shook his head calmly.

I could hardly see any daylight now and I turned my head to the clock that hangs on the wall. It's eight thirty and suddenly all those awful feelings in my head have all awoken once again and I cannot believe that I have slept for over ten hours and without a care in the world. I get up and look at the clothes on the floor once again and Ma's veil's in assorted colours. I pick up the purple shaded one, it has a dark dusky thing about it and quickly I take my own one off my head and firmly leave it with Ma's clothes. It's wet from where I have chewed it for so long but Ma's is perfectly clean and yet dark just like the ink on those rubber stamps. I put her veil on my head, fully covering all my head now for the first time ever and wrapped the long bits around my neck and head. Father looked on. I feel like crying as I have betrayed her just like the voters today.

I have slept for so long and so has she now and

I didn't like her sleeping whilst I was left alone so, how can she be happy with my sleeping for such a long time? I have disappointed her I know, sleeping, not giving her new fresh clothes, her comb, yes that was important as I don't want anyone brushing her hair, she only combs her hair and only I know what make up she wears. Different colours for different moods, hints of darkness to rays of lights and forgotten days of blue shades to the precious days where we talked all day long, amidst the green shades, times spent alone to precious times with Papa, they were her best times and ideally, I wasn't in that equation. She yearned for him like the plant to water as if her well was dried out. She lived with him and for him, but left with nothing except with that emptiness still inside of her.

A quick dash to the bathroom and then I run downstairs but as soon as I get to the bottom step, father is already there waiting, the almighty knower of my little mind. Still with Mother's veil tightly hugging my neck and head and the soggy dove soap still stuck in my left thumb nail. No one's going to look in my nail but then there's the smell of food as well, yes I still have the food in my right fist but I know I have cleverly wrapped it in some lavatory paper as it was seeping out from the middle because of my sweaty hand, it was falling out a bit so I thought that if I wrap it up, it will stay together and fresh for longer.

He stands there like the giant waiting to stop Jack reaching the beanstalk, his big arm grabs me by my waist and my hand is still clutching the big morsel of food waddled in tissues. He stands still even though I can feel my heart beat all the way from the stomach, into the belly button and all the way up to the top of my chest. It is thumping hard. He looks at me straight into my eyes, he takes my hand and slowly wipes away my tears. His left arm slowly sweeps me into the sitting room and it is almost as if he carried me hurriedly and bolted me in so that I could not escape. He made me sit right next to him.

He kept looking at me but I kept looking at the floor, the rug so colourful, the big rose in the middle with its black poignant points triggering like soft dead dry twigs just about to fall off, almost. I look up at Father; his neck also has that same soft dead dry black mole, whats the purpose of that and this. It's carefully placed under his left cheek bone where it's clear to see. It's almost as if they were both so useless and in the wrong place or at least not serving a purpose. What purpose is there for these things, all useless like this aching within me? It's almost as if that black spot is stuck in my throat and its poison is slowly seeping down my throat into a black hole that maybe he made for us. Maybe it's man made and not god made.

I tried to get up and go to Mother but he whispered to me that she has been taken from the spare room. I show him the food that she hasn't eaten but he reminds me that she no longer has a need for it. I interrupt him by saying that I was going to get Ma's clothes, make up and her comb for her and he reassured me that all those things Kaka and Sultana got and she was appropriately done up, and yes, her luscious locks were combed, not brushed and tangle free, he said he remembered. She always combed her long hair in front of him he said and she always slapped her hair to dry it from side to side, then rubbed the towel on it and then combed it, he insisted that it was done exactly like that. Whilst finding it really hard to coax the words out, I asked what she wore on her dusky smooth feet, hands and lips to which he uttered "sweet nothings". Nothing on her gorgeous feet but her favourite red lipstick on her pouted lips, brick red colour was carefully smoothed over as she liked it.

"But she must be cold there, all by herself Papa I have to go to her." Quickly he put his hand over my right hand and I felt that heat from his hand and my own and into the food parcel I had. He was spoiling the food in my fist. I took my hand away from underneath his. He was no fool, he knew, so quickly he slipped his big hand over my left hand. I could feel his blood running through his small fingers almost as if it was going into mine, it made my little finger twitch. With my right hand, I used my thumb to scratch and relieve that twitch which went all the way into my left leg. My foot felt movement and in a sudden movement I rubbed my foot back and forth. There was no real relief but then I was looking for it in the wrong place.

I could not see through the wetness in my eyes. Its blindness was delightful in its own way, as I would rather not see anything than not see her again and she had gone without even eating and when will she. I sat and cried and cried and cried and he promised to make things better in the morning for me, as it was too dark to take me and show me my mother for the final time. I kept uttering the same words "now" and he kept saying "tomorrow". I kept crying, he kept watching, I dozed off without realizing in amidst the tears and the pain and he stayed and put my head on his lap and my legs onto the lifeless sofa. He helped me to purr myself off to sleep just like the big fat fluffy cat, the dead weight against the plank as he sat and I slept all night beside him and no signs of any food in our stomachs, but I still had some held in my hand.

My eyes can see the orange bright colour of the sun shining through and as I squint my eye. I peer from the corner of my eye and see the dead black cat with the green shining emerald eyes sitting in front of the open door. She plays her game well and really isn't any bother to anyone and her dead stony weight is a perfect door opener. She does meow silently and my inner senses can hear her but no one else can. She forever wears a gloomy smile and she has sat there forever and yet I have never slept here before, but today was not an ordinary day. I closed my eyes and lay there lazily just enjoying the golden moment. Thinking back on it as a little girl I used to quickly slide in between my parents in the early house of the morning as we all three would cuddle up in a big bed, perfect family.

Both of them with their backs to one another and yet when I get in and they both face me, cuddle me and yet not to one another in front of me. Two of us always wanting to feel safe and the Master himself made us feel safe and secure but I don't know why she wasn't one of those pages that had much written on it. I wanted to stay asleep forever there and once I started going high school, I don't know how or why, but automatically I still went to their bed, but slept on Mother's side near the edge and yet she always would know that I had come in as she looked through her closed motherly eyes. She could sense the moment that I had stepped into the room as she always said that a mother can sense these things. She would always pull up the duvet and quietly I would slide in like a snail to its shell.

All that had stopped now and how innocent it all was. Mother was Malcolm in the Middle, I was always on the left end of the bed with father on the right side with his back to us and dead to the world. We would sleep, whisper and share lullabies and yet he was the one who was always at peace. We both moved around, wriggled under the sheeted duvet, shared intimate conversations whilst our feet searched the bed sheet and our eyes busily awaited the restful sleep.

"Kaka, can you get the breakfast on the table as the mourners will arrive quite soon and make sure that the rooms are clean and crisp and with only white cloth on the floor and perfectly scented like the way Rani always had the house." I looked up at Kaka, he stood there with a firm nod to acknowledge what has been said and I carefully read the grief on his forehead. Some people spend a lifetime with a family and yet they never are more than just a part of the furniture, quite dead and still from inside and then there are those who in an instance will make their mark and earn their space and respect within the family. Today is that day for Kaka and then there are those like me who never truly understand why someone makes themselves a part of someone else's family and there are people like Kaka who has enjoyed his life with us. You see he has no real family.

Father uttered, "Meera dearest, that clenched fist of yours needs to be emptied, not eaten though. I suggest that you get up, have a quick shower, change your clothes and then we will have breakfast together. Apart from that...."

He was about to continue when I quickly interrupted him "Papa can we go and see mama first, that's much more important than eating?"

"At least go and freshen up and a shower will clear your mind. Today is another long day Meera, and you must eat, keep your energy up and what the hell is all this veil about? You never wore it before and all of the sudden you're turning into a replica of Rani. She never did wear it in bed but even when you are asleep your head is telling you to keep that thing on and you are too young to be obsessed with all of this, just be free, single and stay being a girl not a woman."

I didn't wait for him to carry on so I just got up made sure my veil was firmly still on, almost stuck on with thick hairspray and the food firmly still in my left hand. Quickly he grabs my attention as I slowly look on the floor and he looks at my feet. He raises his eyebrows, thick and long and a bit untamed, sharp at the edges "put your sandals on the right way around." For a moment I continued to look at my feet. Then I started to fumble nervously with the veil and then with a slight tremor in my body, I look at the crumbling food in my hard.

"No, no, no. I have to see mama right now!" I shouted and he looked on at my startled behaviour. He held my hand and took me to the back of the house where mama last lived and all the while, I was wishing that she would be there waiting as her old self again. The woman that was always waiting upstairs in her bedroom, the one who would fumble and twiddle through the images of all the clothes, the one who would now stand in front of the window taking in deep breaths of the scented rose petal candles and as she would breathe out loudly, a fresh smell of the outdoors would breathe within her. She would smile and yet her eyes would not, no, at times her eyes were almost glazed, not empty and lonely all the time, but there was this layer of thought that never truly came down. Father pushed the creaky heavy door open and started to unfold the story of how she was bathed and dressed up in her favourite clothes and make up and then, six men including father carried

72

her on a small bed as she made her farewell journey, to the piece of land where all our ancestors are laid to be burnt down in to nothing. From the soil we rise and to the sod we fall.

The big pyre of logs huddled mother and more were criss-crossed over and around and a dollop of diesel was dropped around, circling her beautiful being and then father himself set a match to its strike. He carried on by telling me that now there is only ash and bones left and when I am ready, I can go, with father to gather these and put them into a copper urn and then, we can both spread the ashes or even float the urn in a river of our choice. A way of setting her soul free and that word free, sounds so good and a word that she did not want to be a part of. My stomach was churning over because it was free from food and that didn't really feel good at all. Am I free now, was I free before but then, I am a little confused as to what is free anyhow?

To think of her, all five feet eight inches high fighting against a six feet tall male, dissolved away into a brass ornamental thing and yet, I am left wondering if the ash will be grey with hints of white as it should be or, will it be red and burning with rage. Dark tint of dusk overshadowed the sky, maybe a resemblance of the real her and the hidden tragedies within her. This room was the same room and yet today it looks empty and yet all the goods were still here except for the one that my heart was searching for. He kept telling me that he was taking me on the same journey that she had taken, and because I missed it all, he was trying to give me a real feel of it now and hopefully would be able to put some of the jigsaw puzzle pieces together.

"Did you cry, Father? Actually I have never seen you cry Papa. Did you cry, do you know the word 'cry'?" I kept on repeating and repeating and repeating to myself, almost as if I had lost my mind and I don't know why I kept repeating for he had heard me the very first time. But that devil inside of me wanted to hurt him for the pain he had caused her, and for him to feel the pain and he didn't cry then and I'm sure he didn't feel the pain as he should have. The same depth of pain that lived within her. Slowly I saw his right hand come close to my lips. I closed my mouth tight. I could smell his hand, it still smelt of some smelly hand cream, he looked deep into my eyes and I looked at him.

'"Hush Meera, hush, please calm down as you are going to make yourself sick child and yes I did cry Meera. In fact, I have never cried since my own mother died when you were very young. I loved your mother and she loved me and I have only loved two women in my entire fifty years, my mother Bella and your mother Rani, that's it Meera," said Father.

I added, "I wish I was on the logs with her papa to keep the fear away from her and she must of been so alone it's all my fault. I stayed with her till the end and I wasn't with her when she needed me to share her pain, I was out of it, that's selfish. I wish I could have taken her place, she loved you dearly father, so dearly that she would rather had had you than me any day. I wish.... I wish.... I was."

"No Meera, no one can take the place of anyone and when it's our time, then so be it. That time is no one else's and Meera, your mother and I, love you very much, so very much and never doubt that ever," he said.

I snapped, "You didn't love her you only loved the politician inside yourself, she wasted all of her life waiting for you, not the man in power but you couldn't give her the one thing she needed, a bit of your undivided attention, a bit more of your precious time."

I could see Kaka in the small washing room now as we both strode along to the field where she was waiting for me. I could see Kaka holding the iron in his right hand and yet looking at us. He was silently sliding the big heavy coal iron with ease and even though I was far from him, I could hear the silent sizzling iron that Kaka forgot to turn on as his mind was elsewhere and as he idly moves, his hand in no motion at all and his eyes are fixed on us both and his mind fixed on the thoughts that were million miles away. A million miles away is where she is now, in body and in soul and as for us, we three are still right here, right now, and I know that I am not going to be alive for that long. I know I will meet her soon enough and I have this gut feeling that it will be sooner rather than later. As we both pass the washer room now, he stands like the cat that always lays dead against the hard dead wooden door, keeping its body parched and still and yet, without any words it is saying so much. He has made no sound or movement. They have something in common.

I try to walk respectfully now, with grace and dignity like she did and now that father has my hand firmly in his tight grip, somehow I feel soothed almost as if my heart has found its original home, but I don't want to feel this way. I don't need him as it isn't good to be needy and more now than ever before, she was a bit like that, but then she never really had him the way she wanted. What chance is there that he will fulfill my needs. 'Dignity, honour and respect' the three important words that always came out of both of their mouths. Honorable child for an important father, I make sure that my veil is still perfectly sitting on my greasy head. That's respect! He leads me from that room to the courtyard as we both quietly walk along and then, through the big ten feet high gates we go into the open allotments that belong to all the locals.

He carries on guiding me to the place where there will be only disappointments waiting for me and I am expecting the outside people to be there scattered around minding other people's business, but far from it as there is hardly anyone here except the big sun and he's bigger than all of us put together. In the background there is a farmer attending to his massive allotment which seems to be laying barren, now a bit like me, dry cracked pencil thin pleats of opening in the ground due to the dry season. He looks up and notices us and just waves at father and carries on. No one is really bothered and yet when they are, we are irritated. One thing for sure though, no one really cares and it doesn't affect anyone else. I can hear children playing in the distance, laughter in their eyes with sweet chattering of nothing on their lips and the echoes of silent whispers when they see us. I know they are talking about us, but it is fine for them as they have had many situations themselves and some of them have mothers to go home to whereas others have never had that luxury. They dance around one another, but now, without the loud mutters and their irritating glances, deep down inside I feel jealousy. It is a bit unbearable but I should not be selfish, but I only wish for my pain to be less and this aching to be numb.

Maybe it will stop when the world ends as many a time intelligent people have predicted that the world will end on so and so date, but I am still here and so I hope that next time they will get it right. The mosquitoes have smelt the humans as I fan my hands to keep them away but father still walks on. We come to a big field and it is pretty empty except for the big mango tree that sits like a gentle giant offering its shade to everyone. It has thick big branches with luscious green thickness and offers free fruit for all and then I see a whole area that is burnt away and just beside it, lays a part of me. I do not need to wonder or ponder, as we both take an extra step towards it and we stand, side by side in grief, uttering no words and yet I can feel what he is trying to say.

I deliberately turn my back to father as I cannot bare to see his face retelling me the event but, I stand beside him as I don't want there to be any distance between us. He doesn't utter a word but I can feel what he is trying to say right from somewhere in my head all the way to the end of my fingertips. The aching inside somewhere in the belly makes me ignore the dry burnt space near my feet so instead, I look at his feet and he looks on. He stares with a fixation on that one spot while I am fixated with his eyes which have narrowed and his eyebrows have not arched, instead he has a droopy look. Could I assume that he is sad? This face of his bares less pain even today than the one I used to see on her face often.

As a child I have played in these fields with the other children, legs crossed and bums perfectly molded on the hard mud ground and the small poor chattering mouths gossiping about the rich him and her and everything on the outside and inside. I don't know why we were infatuated with what our grown-ups got up to and no matter how hard I try, that picture of her in my own head, where she is fumbling through the wardrobe, colours and pastels along with the browns blues and green and yet as she hums along. She remains dusky. Even though it is inappropriate right now, but you can imagine that I am wondering what colour she is showing the world up there now. I stare at fathers hand as he gently grabs me by my right hand and slowly but kindly, tries to make me look where he was looking. I am stubborn, maybe a little like him. There is a little part of me that is a constant reminder of her. He knows that I won't do as I am told right now, so he puts his feet close to mine, I have to move mine back and I notice how his brown skin in smokier than mine, but that is not right for she was darker than him but today, he is smokier than me and why is it that I a lighter than them both. Everything if unfair.

He kept pushing me gently and nudging me forward but without uttering a single word I kept moving backwards. I didn't want to see what was blindly in front of me but, I can see the hair on his back sticking up, so I know he is stressed and through his white top, I can see many shades of black and silver and the big oval line of tan where his stringy white Debenhams vest normally rests. His black flip flops are now tainted with grey ash dust. I don't like grey and especially today and I think that in future I shall never like it or wear it. His big toes are clean and yet there are hints of grey particles, he doesn't shake it off. His top makes tiny movements where his heart has started beating faster and I watch him closely as he rubs his finger in between the space between his nose and moustache. Slowly he slides the finger from the left to the right and we all know that that is his thinking mode and as always, he will follow with a few wise words, "Well, well." There is a silent pause and even the outside world has nothing to offer at this time. "Well Meera, here are the remains of your mother, do you need time by yourself or do you want me to stay, I know, you come back when you are ready in your own time Meera, and I will go back to the house and get breakfast started."

"Am I a burden to you Father, but then you don't need to answer it, otherwise why would you want to leave me now and be here all by myself," I asked.

"Dearest Meera you are never all by yourself. You always have me and I am always going to be here for you and even though your mother may not be here is person anymore, she is very much a part of us even now. Forever in our hearts and sole, for she will remain in our blood for always no matter what. We will never want to rid of that ever," he declared wise words to the ear that were deafened to all reasoning and then through the streaming tears.

"Anyway, Father, what is the point of her being here in spirit and not in person, what is the point of all of this and what is the point of having this big ache that just doesn't seem to go and this heart that is yearning for her and yet it'll never find any consolation and as for her running through our blood, it's made me think that did she bleed and was there pain did she scream or cry did she twitch like I do at times and did her lipstick-colour smear from the sides of his lips or did the blood silently stream from the corner and did her beautiful skin start crumbling......."

"Stop it Meera, she was resting peacefully." He

continued to explain and I continued to think and yet my head was absent and empty as I stood silent and still almost as if, my heart was not beating any more but then, I could still feel her within every bit of me and all her words were embedded in my own vocabulary and all my visions of her were in the forefront. She lay in front of me and even though I am looking at her remains, it is almost as if she is here right now looking like the real princess she was. I open my eyes widely and look at the ground and search for her, yes she is everywhere around me. I couldn't see her but I could smell her and it was almost as if she had gently stroked the back of my neck with her little finger and a quick shudder ran through the small hairs on my back. I looked around as my eyes searched for her frantically and this feeling was so real and yet, my vision was quite clear because I was standing on this grey powdered floor and strange as it may seem, I was treading on her and I even found some motherly warmth within this dusky warm ash.

Chapter 4

I don't know how long I sat on that mushroomed-smelling gravelly floor and as the sense of time had really been outstretched but then, the sun was still smiling and the sky was as the bright sky should be. The air was soothingly warm and soft as if there were no pollutants spoiling it and even though I couldn't see much more than that, apart from the ever so menacing flutters of the ugly butterflies. The dark dangerous mosquitoes in their small groups were trying busily as ever to pass on their filth, to yet another victim and the big bold black flies parading themselves into the clear sky, whilst leaving behind their trail of germs and disease, almost unseen by the human eye. But where all those who were just like me?

Father's last words to me kept echoing in my ears against the tiny speckles of hair as if he was repeating them continuously in my ear, but he has already left my side to give me space to mourn and time to get to grips with the new reality. He told me to come back when I was ready. I have always hated that word 'ready' as when the hell is anyone ever really ready for anything as it's always left to him upstairs? Some just use that word as it means a great deal to their routine, as others like me are told to put that in to context within our life and yet, know very little about the word itself in a disastrous situation.

No one I feel is ever truly ready for anything, a

new born is never ready to be born, a toddler is put into walkers to encourage mobility even though it may not be ready to as yet, children at times are not ready to eat and yet mothers force feed their young ones with pale tasteless baby food in plastic dressed up colourful plates and spoons. Those who pretend to make the rules; the adults themselves don't tow that line of being ready as well. Women who have to pretend to be ready for getting married to someone that parents choose and then to become parents and become maternal animals even though they may have never been ready. They have to conform to that idea of what and when people need to be ready. Men who always have to be ready to go out to work to financially support their families leaving them under great stress and pressure and it goes on and on. Fathers ready to leave the house in hurry and mothers always ready for his return and I am forever 'ready' for absolutely nothing!

I don't know how long I sat there next to her, within her soul but without her, the grey smoky earth trodden over by my feet and the weight of my body as I sat criss-crossed against her remains. The only thing missing was the colour of her veil. There was no red amongst the grey but mine was still guarding me. some people talk to the living trees and not to the dead bark, others talk to the flower rather than to the stem and then there are those of us, who prefer to talk to others like ourselves, but there is no one who can actually and physically hear us and we cannot simply find the words from the dumb mouth for the deaf ears.

There was no plan in my own mind what so ever and even though I was sitting on the ash one minute, but the next moment I was actually standing where the outside people stood. It felt good to be free like them, now I had to think like them and be street wise for the first time ever, and so, I just stood and observed. The picture within the bigger picture of this grand long road stood still for no one, flurries of minute tingles of rain droplets give fine crystal speckles to drop on my softly dampened nose. I should have felt free and full of life but the veil captured the old life and I didn't want to be free from that. I owed it to her.

I stood with the veil covering not only my head but neck as well and if there were a mirror in front of me, it would have spoken about the woman, not the girl. Battered cars zoom by; taxis heralded down by the needy passengers whilst the outside people move ever so slowly like the tea leaves in a stormy tea cup. The election fever is still ripe and the voters are nowhere to be seen. The winners looting the streets, drunken cans emptily roll around, the yobs kicking the litter with their half-naked feet and the jubilant are out, arm in arm walking by with their loud voices. Drivers and passengers in their cars, passing by with dignity and stopping at the huts to buy sweet sugary milk drinks and savory snacks. There are hardly any females within these jubilant crowds and it's perfectly acceptable to be arm in arm with the same sex and even the 'yes sir, yes sir' people are all mainly males. Where are the women and what roles are they playing now?

Sultana, and all the outside people and Mimi as well, sweet little nothings that people have forgotten about. A policeman is slowly gathering pace as he comes close to where I am standing, I pull my red veil half way down to cover my left cheek and the corner of my nose and bite the cloth tightly with my lip. This one doesn't have a beer belly as I closely look at his tight stomach whilst he clears his throat. I look into his eyes and he kindly utters "Alright, lady?" I don't recognise him and nor does he know that in fact, I am a dweller of one of these bungalows and I want to feel proud and tell him but, its far better just watching him. His gaze narrows and his eyebrows arch and I fear of being recognised as one of the inside people, it haunts me and then he utters in a soft warm tone, "It's dangerous walking bare-footed, lady."

Without even moving my head, my eyes quickly look down at my feet, he was right and then I offer something in return, my left hand comes up and I open my palm. "Would you like to eat some food," he looks smugly now. Maybe he's not as nice as he looks because, he speaks with a lot of thought but not a lot of words.

"You've eaten what was in your hand lady, there are only crumbs remaining but don't worry dear." Quickly he puts his thumb and forefinger in his shirt breast pocket and takes out some money and puts it on the crumbs. "You must be hungry lady, buy yourself something nice to eat." Without even thinking I quickly replied, "I don't need money I have lots." And he rudely interrupted, "Of course you do lady but of course you do, I can tell by looking at you, here's looking at you kid!!"

"Do you know who has won the elections?" I asked enquiringly and with that he starts to nod his tiny head stuck on the massive boned, rectangular face.

"Elections, yes of course, a few winners and some losers but then they are all the same, in it for themselves really, but why do you ask, it doesn't affect you or me lady."

My mouth opened, I said, "Well actually it does affect me because my father is or was the chairman and member of the local parliament and I don't know if he has won or not this time around."

He rudely snapped "Of course lady, of course your dear father must be closely related to our prime minister right, of course how silly of me not to have recognised you, utter rubbish. Honestly the elections have created so much chaos, rioting and turbulence everywhere, we've been patrolling around the town for days now trying to keep the peace, a waste of our very little resources and time that we don't have. You know lady, I should be spending that time with my new lady wife, rather than out on the streets and the new missus is not happy about that, as I have not been home much in the last four days. You don't know, and how could you know, that she isn't much older than you. You know she's younger than me and all that but you know what 'second time round' means? Well, got to keep the lady happy, right lady?"

"I am not a lady, I am a school girl still and I have not slept properly in days either and happy, well, I don't even know the meaning of that right now and second wife, is your wife happy. I don't know about that as my father has only one wife, my mother and....." There was a long pause and then a cold harsh reality check went through my mind.

"Does that mean that he'll take another wife?" I asked him. I felt confused and disillusioned as my eyes strayed. "Why would he, I presume you're talking about your father taking another wife when he's already married to your mother. I married coz my first love died." That word DIED rung so many sad tunes in my head as I shouted, "So has she?!" He looked a little startled at the outburst and his bemused smile erased from his face.

"Yes lady, of course she has died in your little imagination and that's why you're out here enjoying life and celebrating the elections and all the excitement and of course to top it all up, you are going to tell me how you and your father live in one of these fine fancy rich houses, right? By the looks of you, you do look like a classy act, what drama was this story from as we Asians love our dramas, by the way what drama is this story from that you have just told me. Listen lady, do yourself a favour and scarper from here. A very poor excuse for watching the elections drama. I suggest you go and watch it on someone's TV as it will be much more peaceful as well, now hop along!"

His shiny black pointy shoes strike the floor the same time as his baton strikes his hand gently, his shoes move along, they must be at least a size ten and I am only a size six myself. He continues with long stride and within his path many have moved to make way for him and his controlling baton. Boys stop kicking the trash bucket and stand like perfectly-mannered soldiers, a mother walks by with her junior child, no more than ten, and he salutes the policeman with a big grin. "Behave son" she tells him and he is out to please her but when he passes the policeman, he puts his tiny hand into his trouser pocket and all of a sudden he smiles. He has found the chewed gum and quickly puts it back into his tiny mouth. The saliva dribbles and the his mother hurriedly tries to shove her finger into his mouth to scrape out the gum, but the more that she insists, the more he tightens his top molars with the bottom ones. He knows he has won. There is a dull smack that she plants onto his back and I see the top of her long nail tip and I stare, but she is not swayed by anything. She holds his hand tightly as they peacefully walk on.

How magical and peaceful everything looks compared to my world. I know, the air seems fragranced with the plants, humans and the animals and the wind seems jovial slowly singing along and it feels as if these people are all living and there is life in all and everything. My legs seem tired and even though I did sleep, but I know I have not eaten, the life inside of me cannot be bought with the money the policeman has given me. He is not as old as Colombo or as young as magnum but looks a little like Kojak, minus the fact that he didn't flirt, didn't suck a lollypop and had masses of hair unlike Kojak.

Thinking of hair, I don't know why, but here men tend to have a full head of hair, maybe it's the heat or the oil! I feel that I cannot give him a name as he doesn't fit perfectly in to any one person, perhaps he could remain as police constable. This deems to be real life and there is some innocence in him and I feel somewhat proud to be a part of life today. I had not seen this part of life before and I had not been out like this all by myself and never bare-footed. I have always had a chaperon, someone who always looked out for me in the form of school, friends, Mother, Father or Kaka and yet today there was no need for any of them or me.

I am aware that I am standing quite close to my own bungalow and know that father would not be watching me but what if someone else recognises me. I do have this veil on me still, maybe no one will and I do really like it here. This outside world for the fortunate outside people who are allowed to breathe free. He thinks that I am still in the back, away from harm and all these people and this world and I do not know what he would think or say if he knew where I was. There is a girl standing near the bus stop. As I carry on walking bare-footed away from home and in the opposite direction of my school, she is wearing a very thin pale yellow worn out cotton suit. Her hair is nearly waist length and a shade of sun damaged earthy brown old fudge and it does look quite nice and it is not in plaits like most have it here. It hangs like a beautiful tail and when she sees a male walking past her, she gets her scarf and quickly covers her head a little and as soon as the male has past she takes it and puts it around her neck.

There is a living fear in her as well and I can tell that just by the way that she nips and tucks at the corners of the scarf with her tiny thin fingers. She has her right hand tucked in to the pocket of her dress and gently she rocks her body in a swaying motion from side to side. She is not a Leo like me or maybe society has not allowed her to be and she is not aggressive but the hidden assertiveness is dug inside. Don't they say that same star signs get on better? Maybe I won't get on well with her, but then, I am not looking for a friend for a while. I need them, but for long-term who I can rely on and definitely not the outside people.

I go and stand next to her and copy what she does. The veil is still on, the money that's on the crumbs in my palm is still there and I put the other hand on my hips as I don't have a pocket like her. She keeps looking at me and whispering under her breath, 'never seen a girl before' and in a coy manner she keeps a watchful eye on me from the corners of her eyes and doesn't really talk to me and I do the same. Maybe she thinks I am lost or that we are the same, both lost on this far horizon and outsiders at that. She stops muttering and asks if I am lost and I say no. She asks if I am waiting for someone or the bus and I shake my head. She looks at me and asks where I am going, and I shake my head again. She plucks up courage and asks if I am going NOWHERE. I can hear the rude cars driving and honking and many buses have come and gone, picking the passengers and driving off to their desired destinations. Somehow that word "nowhere" sounded really intriguing and even though I took many moments to think about it, finally I did nod and all of a sudden it was as if this was not the same girl any more. She smiled and nodded herself and asked "Shall we go nowhere together?" We look at one another as I nod again and there was this big weight being lifted off my shoulders and a breath of something new within.

Apart from the journey to nowhere we had something much more in common, we were both barefooted. There was a small rocky wall behind the bus stop and she decided that we were both tired and it would be great to sit on that and take in life. So quickly sliding her body onto it she sat comfortably with her feet dangling down. No wonder her clothes were worn out because of the rubbing against harsh surfaces and I could tell she was used to it. I couldn't climb or slide on and then she stood up and pulled me up and then we both sat and watched the passers-by.

She told me her name was Marilyn and I just

nodded. She then said it was Marilyn Monroe and I didn't react at all so she started to explain that her real name was Rania but everyone called her Rani for short and my head started questioning as to whether mother's real name was Rani or Rania, but Rani was a proper name all by itself. I don't know how or why but as soon as she started telling me her name the only thing I saw was mother in front of me, so rudely I told her my name was Madonna. Rani the Princess and then there is this girl no more than eighteen. She could have also been a princess of the slum world and yet my own rani was a figure of a real beauty. My lips smiled and she quickly watched my words and the empty expression, sunken wide smile still pasted on my face.

I started telling her about my mother and how her name was the same and quite abruptly she replied, "Huh, of course." And with that she started rabbiting on about her adventurous and the life where she is the main bread winner of the family and her parents' only child. They call her the son of the house because she fulfills the roles of the son in every way she can. Her parents were old and she would leave home first thing in the morning and return last thing at night but, always before dark and all day she spent hunting the vulnerable and kind, emotionally manipulate a few and of course beg, steal or pretend to borrow, and as long as she had something to show her parents when she got home and not just her child like face or her empty pockets, or her hands that hadn't done an innocent days work. She had to take something worthwhile for the day.

I asked her why she kept her hand firmly in the pocket all the time and a coy smile ran through her petite lips. She asked why I had mine on the hip and the other tightly closed. I managed half a smile and told her that I was copying her but didn't have a pocket, so the hip was near enough and as for the closed fist, it had food in it. Quickly, without thinking or waiting, she said I should share my food with her, so I opened my palm and she asked where the food was. I looked at her and then at my palm and then at her high cheek bones and she had not had a good feed in ages. She raised her eyebrow and impulsively and uttered mockingly that crumbs were not going to fill anyone up and especially two hungry mouths. Her eyes lit up as she saw the money in my hand, as she said, "We could get quite a lot with that."

Quickly we both got off the rugged wall whilst ripping my top in the process as it got caught in the cracks of the stones and we headed off to the nearest food stall. We brought her favourite foods, and her "bestest" ever drink, sugar cane juice straight from the long hard sugar cane itself, peeled, chopped and forced through, to make her perfect drink slumped straight into a tall, somewhat dirty stained glass and a used but rinsed straw dunked into it. The look on her face showed that this glass of delight had reached her heavenly senses and it was not the first time that I had this drink either. I didn't eat much but she ate and drank most of it. We spent all the money I had and she was content. She said she normally doesn't buy food for herself as she keeps the money to give to her mother and any food that she gets given to her, she wraps it in to her scarf and takes it home to save mother from wasting energy. What a different and delightful hearty felt world this outside world really is, a world of caring and sharing and of giving and taking.

A lot of time must have gone by but I was totally unaware of it all and as she finished her food and we roamed the back streets of the slum where I had not trodden on before. She showed me all the places where she had made money. I kept looking at her other hand as she had it safely in her pocket still and as she became quite aware of the fact that I was looking. A slight chuckle came from her within her throat as she replied that she had often cut out people's pockets and so, when she has money, her hand stays with it. With this we both rolled out in laughter to imagine a young lady a real pick pocket standing sheepishly with a tiny scissors in her empty pocket and slowly edging towards a full pocket and in next to no time, Rani's pocket is full. She asked where I was from, as she had never seen me in the streets before.

I went on to explain that I lived here in the Rani bungalow on this big road to which she laughed and said that she was indeed a real princess. I then told her that she must go to this bungalow and ask for money and then she will know, but she insisted that I must have been there and got money from the owners and that is why I am saying this. I didn't nod or reply because she only had faith in her own words. She trusted no one. Suddenly, there was a flutter of sweet earthy-smelling rain drops and the cars started speeding, others slowed down, some parked up the kerb and the outside people disappeared almost into the air and then there was Marilyn and I standing together. We looked into each other's eyes and there was a sly twinkle in hers. Suddenly we both took off our veils and tied them around our waists and with our arms stretched out wide and in full with our heads looking up at the pouring heavens. Our delighted bodies twirling around to the sound of popular dance music, oozing out from the broken speakers in the nearby shop.

We shook our hair as it laid limp against our clothes and I could see that she wore no under garments as her clothes clung really tightly against her and her feet looked sore and red from all her hard work. "You'll catch your death girls, get under cover somewhere" was all that everyone chanted. The shopkeepers told us to go into their shops for cover and some just made small gestures with their hands for us to follow them, but of course we ignored them all until the rain had run out of all of its energy. The sun was still peeping through the cracks of the rain and the rain felt invigorating against our bodies, slow luscious bearable pain that had an enjoyment all of its own.

The sun still bright and tantalizing and the rain

95

against its glow felt so invigorating and alive like the musical ears against the beating drum. Our feet were muddy now and everything else wet to the core and yet the sky was now quickly dry and still almost as if the last episode didn't take place. There were slight tremors of the darkness in the air on the backdrop of the far horizon, but in my heart it felt wonderful and it was then that I realized that in fact it was actually getting dark and the night was trying to draw itself in. It was time to face real life and I had a whole day to live like the outside people and it was a real beautiful eye opener, it was real life but then my mother would have wanted me to be at my father's side by now and so that is what I must do.

I told Marilyn I needed to go now and she said that we must both part in our ways but meet again tomorrow and every day after that, but I told her I do live in the Rani bungalow and that I won't be coming again and certainly not like this. She laughed and said that she understood the need for me to make believe this fantasy life and how dreams are really important and more so, to believe in them, otherwise life is just an empty closet and the need for wanting things to be true is vital and how only the survivors have it in them to be able to make up lies as she does, all the time.

Dreams always come true she said and then a big smile and a proud faced Marilyn paused and gave a big chuckle. "So you think that you can fool me by telling me that story again and again. I know you are like us, you look like us and I knew straight away when I saw you, bare-footed and all, even I don't come out bare often and today, I came because my sandal broke and Mother wouldn't give me money to have it mended. She said I could wear something else and Father will repair it whilst I am at work. You wait and see girl how I will be wearing them tomorrow and how wonderful they will look. They will look new and not tattered and mended and mother and I share ours any way. There is only one or two size difference between us.

"Why not just buy another pair?" I asked.

"Buy Madonna? You of all people know that we don't have the luxury of buying for ourselves but I often buy for my parents and whenever I am buying for Mother, I try and get her something rather special. And even though our tummies may often be empty, the feet should look great. It spells out quality like Marks and Spencers. As for my own, I don't really care, but hers I do care a lot about and for me, I only run around in them and spoil them. So spending on her sandals and my make-up, that's important.

"Make-up?"

"Make-up and perfume, that is, and obviously I cannot afford channel perfume but the box and bottle, I must have those expensive boxes with imitation smells, I know, even I know what's what."

"It's Chanel," I burst her bubble and in a cocky way she barks back.

"That's what I said, channel." I smiled and then

asked what she buys the make for and when does she ever get to wear it and the perfume would be wasted as most people here out in the sun every day smell of sweat not perfume.

"Aha, that's it, that's the point 'coz I only have enough water for a bucket wash regularly and we don't have the bath and shower and there is hardly any water and that is mainly cold and when it's too cold to bear, then I spray the perfume instead and if I caught a chill whilst bathing in the cold water than how would I afford the medicines, huh? Anyhow, the smell of perfume makes me feel worthy, Oh yes, can I ask before you go how come your English is better than mine?"

"How do you know my English is better than yours?"

"Well, you were talking to that guy in the shop and you keep correcting me as well even though I am right, but you just feel you are better, that means that you have worked in a rich man's house and they have taught you."

"Well Marilyn, you won't believe me even if I told you so it's better not to go over that again."

"Aha, it's Marilyn Monroe, not just Marilyn. I am going to be very famous one day just like her and I am going to turn out beautiful just like her as well and then I will go to the Big Apple, the famous Americas, where everything happens and the rich live and just enjoy being famous like Marilyn and Maradona. Who did you say she was, this Maradona?"

"'A very famous singer and it's not Maradona

its Ma-don-na."

"Yeh yeh, that's what I said. I don't know why you get so perfect with your English and anyway, I am sure we will meet again and certainly when we are both rich but for now, if you can get to this area again then we will meet. It's been a fun day; see you round."

"You are indeed Marilyn Monroe and who knows, we may meet again," I replied.

As darkness loomed and the sun was shying away and with Marilyn's back to me and my feet doing the walking, I look around and the outside people are still out doing their everyday things and Maggie is not here today and sultana has probably been and gone and Lakeed and so many others all done their day as I have. I put my hand on the buzzer and I see the grim faces looking at the floor and Kaka watching out of the window waiting for me. The plates he heated but forgot to put the food on and there was no one hungry yet again today and the dinner table with its silver-lined cutlery shining away happily and yet again no one sitting at it. The parcels of food that these residents just didn't want to eat laid idly in the trash and so, I take my hand off the buzzer and quietly go around the back. I stand outside this big gate where the outside people don't come in and I carefully look around.

The lights of the houses are all on but there is a dark feel in the air and there is smell of food dancing around and yet my stomach does not yearn for it. The lights of the houses are all alive but some are dead in body, soul and mind. The creatures and animals are still alive and tamed by their keepers now. There are a few camels stomping home and I can hear the bulls with their clanging bells around their necks, heading home with their masters and the green frogs still looking ugly and croaking away in between the wet damp green marsh and the crickets racketing away and I can hear the hiss of the snake, leering nearby but I do not have to worry about any of them as once I have closed this gate behind me, nothing will come in. I push the big gate open and I turn around and look at where Mother laid one day. I know where it is but I cannot see her and then I close the gate behind me and walk towards the kitchen door.

"Meera, I have been waiting for you dear, the house is warm and scented with your favourite candles and the food plates are warm and waiting for someone to eat from them and of course, your favourite food has been made and placed at the table. Salmon just the way you like it and for dessert, I got the bakery to deliver chocolate cake that you so like, now let's sit and enjoy." I quietly mumbled yes let's sit and eat and then he continued by telling me to wash my hands. I rush off to the big white butler sink and hit the hand wash bottle on the head, the squidgy red zesty liquid soap oozes out and I know I have seen this not so long ago on her and I quickly gather it in my palm. The crumbs have all gone but the nails still show the dirt of the day as I gently rub them together. The big mixer tap bellows out the clear water and then I reach for the fluffy red towel.

I take my place at the table, with Father at the headmaster's seat, cushioned seat and arm and head rest and I sit as always on his left but without the cushioned head rest and then the seat opposite me, the one on the right of father is empty just like his own heart today but before that an empty soul sat on it. Kaka always sat next to mother. Father tells Kaka to sit on the next chair along and without leaving a big hole in our lives and he places his bottom on Mother's chair to create a harmonious atmosphere and like an obedient slave to the master he does exactly that and hangs his head down. Father mutters a quick prayer, as normally with Mother it would always be a long and lengthy affair. Father's habit was always the same, Mother praying and Father dying for the food to be swallowed quicker than quick. But now it's in his control and all I have heard is the beginning and the end and all the bits in between have been forgotten. I pray nothing as it all means very little and far too late now, but I want this to continue as it is a memory of her.

We three ate the food as if we had not eaten in a long while and that was true as well, it felt so comforting not because the food was hot and delicious but simply because, it felt like home after a long time. We gossiped, predicted and annualized a lot of situations at mealtimes. We all talked at the eating table and it was soothing because ma would reply, smile and laugh and we all interacted like a real family should. When

Father was sitting at the table he always had so many stories to tell and all about men and somehow tales about men always seemed more interesting than what women cooked or wore.

Talk of men doing business in the bazaar outweigh women milking the cow in the backyard, big butch men talking about small things like who got beaten up or put under pressure by who and the important things of finance like the price of gold and the exchange rate of the dollar. Ma and I both felt that the conversation was always much more interesting than the "wow" factor behind fashion, make-up and daily domestic chore like shopping. Maybe I should have been born a boy but then there were those traditional female things in me as well like sitting on the window watching life go by. The life that was always on the outside and yet here I am on the inside and women, walking along with their hands on their hips and dirty glasses that they can see through, so they wear them on the tip of their nose and they always walk on the bright side of the fence and here I am still on the dark side where grass is never that green.

Whilst having our food, there was a strange kind of comfort because Father was with us and we enjoyed his company. At breakfast and dinner he ate with us most of the time, but lunch was normally spent with his mates.

"May I speak papa?" I asked.

"Why of course Mimi, go for it, girl," he replied.

And so I did. I retraced my footprints back to

the time early this morning and when we both stepped out of this family house and treaded on the early morning dew, so fresh, unspoilt and clean. It was like stepping onto slushy snow and the crunchiness even though I have never experienced it myself. As I talked about the dew, Father's eyes moved away from his plate onto the wall in front of him and yet there was nothing but the pail looking plaster sugar coated with love. He carefully put his cutlery down and began to eat with his bare hands. He remembered how Mother always reminded him to do justice to the food by feeling the food and respecting it, but only with bare hands.

I continued and tried to get Kaka and Father both to visualise my short time there with Mother amongst the rotten ash. I talked about how I spoke to her and believed, that even though she was listening more to him upstairs, but she most definitely heard everything that I said to her, but there was no reconciliation with her or me or with the situation so, all I could do was cry and that came plentiful. As I sat with the earth beneath me poking into my bones, into my behind and the dry sod marking my clothes and my wondering eyes looking at the ants trying to play connect four between my legs and how they crawled creepily into my clothes and yet, I couldn't even feel them annoying me. It was just them, me and my slippers that stood barren and alone. We all looked worn out, washed out and senseless to the silence around us so I knew I was in the right company. My tears drip drop straight onto the floor and watched my nose doing the exactly the same until I heard her say "Set yourself free."

In an instant I took out my cradled head out of my lap and looked up and now, all I could hear was the sweet sound of the red robin red breast happily chirping away and though I kept asking Mother to repeat, she never did. I knew it was much too late because I had been let loose from her cord and that was what she said and I did. 'What did you do Meera?' asked Kaka quizzingly.

I continued by saying that I got up and it was almost as if I was not actually getting up myself but someone had pulled me up and I simply followed their footsteps by using my inner senses rather than my body. I couldn't see anyone physically or mentally and after a few minutes, I found myself standing alongside Mrs Chaudry's bungalow. Father cut me with that disappointed look in his brow, squinting even further and then came the scolding "You've been told Meera not to use that entrance as a lot of animals, tractors and farmers cross that path and it's full of animal dung and full of roaming wild dogs in search of food."

I rudely interrupted by saying I was fine, but watched Father look at Kaka with his mind working overtime as if he was trying to tell Kaka something, but in silence and yet even though I didn't understand, Kaka certainly did. He raised his right eyebrow and tilted his head a quarter of the way down and then nodded twice whilst hanging his chin down southwards. I looked back at Father and continued and so did the clickety-clack on my plate. I spelt out the wonder and joy of roaming the outside and right here outside my own house and for once, all by myself and not only did I watch life but I had conversations with Police Inspector Nettles.

"Police Inspector Nettles?" Father asked, half-listening.

I insisted that he should listen as I was telling the truth, but by this time he had licked his plate clean and was busy rubbing his black moustache in the direction of the winds from the east to the west with his firm thumbs. Slowly without making it obvious, he slid his big chair a little back to give his full barrel a little more space to breathe. I could tell that he wanted to get up as he always finished first and then, he would hurry everyone to move to the sitting area and there he would slouch into his arm chair. That is what an English gentleman does but he was far from being English. I quickly put my hand on top of his and that is exactly what Mother used to do and with that, he could not get up from the dining table until her hand or mine was no longer touching his.

I explained that 'Nettles' was not his real name and it was a name that I gave him as he was not as old and withered away or in deed young or handsome either. I told them both that we talked and he even gave me money as he thought I looked hungry. He thought I was a beggar girl and no sooner had I said this word, that they were both in fits of laughter. I couldn't see the funny side of this laughter but they could not control theirs. "And as I was saying Papa....." my fairytale continued as they both thought. I told them both about my encounter and friendship with Marilyn Monroe and how we both danced with the rain gods and how we were both drenched and we both told each other about each other's lives and how her life was way more exciting than mine, but for her, mine was fab so she said. She was a true beggar girl, a real cunning crook and small time thief and that was her family's only source of income and then it was getting dark and all the excitement had to come to an end. I know real life is not like that every day, so quickly and quietly, I gathered my life together and rolled back home.

"Well, what an adventure Meera. Really it is, and now if you have finished, we could have coffee in the dining room, if you please."

"You can say whatever you like Papa but it's the truth and just look at my clothes. You can tell they have been soaked and my worn out lifeless sandals are still by Mother's side and look at my hair, it's still or rather it was damp and my veil, look at it father, it was, well it was on my head when I left home and when I went out in the rain, I tied it around my waist and it's still there and damp." With that I hurriedly opened the knots and quickly laid it on the table and the other hand still on Father's hand. I now placed his hand on my veil. "Feel it father, come on feel it. Kaka, you too."

"Meera, dearest Meera, we do believe you

106

when you say you got wet, we do but all this Marilyn goddess Monroe...."

"And I was Madonna for the day and it made me forget everything bad for the day."

"Now listen Meera, please, please." Now with his hands both in the air. "Please child, let's not hear any more about Marilyn and Madonna and of all people. Do you even know who Madonna is? Marilyn everyone knows, but Madonna?"

"Father, you know Marilyn because she's old like you and dead like Ma but Madonna is a super star in England and she has kids and yes, I listen to her songs and she's the one who has that lucky gap in between her top middle teeth and they have bought her good luck."

"Of course you do girl," he said with a big sigh. I carried on with a little song of Madonna's called "Papa Don't Preach". I carried on telling him and he told me to stop preaching but that something had made my mood good and my pain had been masked and that was good enough. This made me raise my voice further which was not allowed in our house. No-one raises their voices here but instead our tones change like the rainbow colours with our moods but there has been no raving or ranting in this civilized household. I carried on with bittersweet words and with the tone that felt trapped within my emotionally muddled-up words, stutters and fumbles. I continued to explain how Marilyn's real name was Rania and was called Rani for short and that she didn't believe me when I told her that I was not a beggar like her but in fact, I lived in these houses and how she grinned and mocked and hissed a slight chuckle by replying that it was so evident, as a rich girl dresses in soaking rags and bare-footed. That did seem to be the perfect picture of who I wanted to be.

No sooner had those words entered his ears that the look on his face changed. His anxious brow no longer narrowed, his wide big lips now curved with a smile on the edges and his eyes pictured a twinkling of that wet dripping bare-footed girl running home to enter the grand gates of his house. I felt his pain from within as if something had touched him and that touched me with the same wave of energy. That smile left his eyes and the width of his lips shortened but his mouth opened a little flatter, but no words came out. He tried again and once again but nothing reached my ears and yet my heart fluttered until I could not only hear my heartbeat, but also hear my own silent voice. What was the sensation and the danger unknown that bound us together and we felt something and those words that could not leave him and my deafened ears that felt something and there was no absolute fear, just an unsure, uncertain flame burning away inside of us both.

Chapter 5

The uncertain burning flame inside of him was busily flickering away as my eyes dropped down like the wax down the candles body after the aftermath of the last month. But it had so many repercussions that we both did not anticipate, but such was life. Some people have that heat burning deep down inside and know its final destination, but then there are those who simply are left without any light at the beginning of the tunnel, let alone at the end. The end for mother was neigh as I gathered her remains from the piece of cracked land and I rewarded her by putting her into a beautiful golden vase and there she lay in a prestigious manner. She was always laden with gold whilst alive and even now it is the gold that has captured her. The vase was beautiful and so was the content, both absolutely priceless.

The artificial burning of the lamp and of her, the beauty adorned of the vase and of her and yet we all three are empty in our ways. I do not really know how empty fathers beating heart is and as for his life, there will not be any real emptiness, I don't think. He will not have that black hole right in the middle of his life, but for us females, that black hole was and still is a big part of reality. Darkness within and still darkness all around. The plates had been scratched clean with only traces of food juices lingering, stomach is so full that dessert was forgotten about and the table that has now sat three rather than four seemed as if it was normal. It all seemed a very long time ago. The cluttering in the butler's sink where Kaka dumped plate on top of plate with the cutlery dropping off the plate and the three glasses tinkered together waiting to be shined again.

For a moment everything seemed to be alive in this house, including us three and as we moved into the comfortable armchairs. Kaka turned the button down of the kettle so that the heated hiss could start as I lazily watched father moving around in the chair so that he could find a comfortable spot. That was it, his legs stretched out till they could reach no further, his stomach resting on his thighs now and his neck armour unseen with the double chin that seems to get bigger when eating. His palms rest on the corners of his armchair as he looks into the clouded space.

"Kaka, where is my paper?" The paper is quietly shipped into his lap and he moves his hands whilst scratching the paper. I can see the circled hand prints left on the armchair. He crosses his legs and starts to read. This was always his time for about fifteen minutes as he looked hurriedly through all of the paper, front to back and as his eyes met with the uncomfortable news of the day. His brows would arch and that squint in his eyes would harden, but he would never not read the whole article. After skimming the stories, he would end up to his favourite part, the politicians and the politics. Both masters of our lives. He was a politician as well and acted like a powerful man and looked the figure as well. The slow walk, hands held behind his back whilst comforting each other and his tall big body upright, a little too much. He walked in his own shadow.

Father has read all of the paper and I have read all of the stories that these not-so-hollow walls have told. It was almost as if time had flown by, as half an hour had passed and within that time, we offered no words to one another but we all shared that golden silence with the flickers of the different story's and the tinkering of the tea cups with decaf coffee, strong and black. The steady slurping and tasting from Kaka's mouth and all I could wish was, when was his coffee going to finish as that noise was indeed louder than us. He refilled his cup and started again and as he sees Father's empty cup, politely he gets up to refill it. Father looks up at him and thanks him for being so prompt and offers a smile and then he sees me watching him.

"Mimi, dear Mimi, shall we all retire to bed now, it's been a long day? Tomorrow will be the same but then I think the masses of people will stop coming and only the selective few who are close to us will come to join in. Prayers for a week or so and then Meera." He breathed in a bid deep sigh and for a moment, his stomach left the thighs and as he breathed out, it rested happily back into its place. He raised his right hand and starts to scratch the back of his head quite harshly as if he is in pain and the deeper his pain, the harder his actions and yet he seemed to be enjoying this pain. Pain is beauty.

He stopped the enjoyment and started to finish off what he had already started. "And then, Meera, we can think about your future but for now, I think that you are ready to go back to school and finish off your exams for the year. You go ahead child and anyhow, it will keep your mind busy and active. It might be good for you, just let Kaka know the night before."

"But father, not yet."

"Fine, fine Meera."

"Okay, okay Papa."

"Shall we all retire to our rooms now, it is rather late?" With these words he stood and moved towards the door. I rose to follow him and I could hear Kaka behind me. Father and I climbed the stairs and then Father goes towards her and his room, and I towards mine and I stand in silence looking all around me. This brightly lit house with grand chandeliers tussling out their lights as if this house has so much life in it and all around it, but that emptiness that I saw in her eyes everyday at some point or other, I can feel in my own eyes now. The big mirror in front of me has shown me that as well and it is, as if I am looking through Rani's eyes. It is not a soothing or warming thought, or a peaceful thought that is cradling me but the opposite. There is an almost terror in my own eyes and yet I do not know why. It is the uncertainty of not knowing about her life and of mine now to begin, as everything has changed even though there was a glimpse of normality in Father's voice tonight. As for Kaka, he's not a blood relative and yet in him I see the absence of my mother. In his nervousness, I can feel the pain of her loss, his smile so warm and yet it has been absent for many days and his chirpy singing voice has made absolutely no sound and instead of us being alive in our own home, it's the outside people who possess the property all day. It is all so real and yet so very uncertain. I do not know what to say and to who or even what to think anymore.

The lights have been turned off by Kaka and only the hall light is left on which spreads its joy in all the main area of the house and this light, has always been so comforting. When you go anywhere in the house, during the night this light is always there for you and even today, it is regular like clockwork. I turn my back towards the light and look to the future where there is shade. I hold the wooden knob of my bedroom door in my right hand as my left hands rests on the golden frame plate and my head peacefully rests next to it. I hold myself there for such a long time and as the tears flow without even resting in between, there is no thought or understanding about why and where these tears have come from and their emotional destination. It was not the time for words what so ever but then, maybe these tears were my words right now. I felt empty and lifeless and when I finally open my door, I can see the clock ticking away to midnight.

With my day clothes still on and my hair feeling

crispy and crimpy, I slowly walk towards my bed without turning the light on and yet leaving the door fully ajar. I slump my stomach onto the bed and pull the fluffy tiger blanket over me all the way over my head. I can feel myself breath underneath my body almost as if my heart was echoing away and yet the blanket carefully shaded all of me within it safely. My eyes are so very happy and sore and so painful to open but then I cannot possibly open them now, even though my feet feel dirty and I want to get up and shake off the dirt from them but, that is not going to happen. It is almost as if I am in the warm jungle fast asleep and the tiger is awake keeping me safe whilst I sleep.

Underneath the darkness of the brown and patchy black tiger I cannot see the morning cracked sunrise or hear the day break glory. But I am aware of what my ears can hear, the rustling of people going up and down the stairs, some with their pointy heels clicking on the floor and others openly scraping their feet forward and then there are those who have those expensive flat-heeled shoes firmly gripping their feet. Normally there would only be three sets of different feet going up and down that the tiger rug that I used to hear but things are gradually changing and so will the footsteps. The jungle is warm and it is safe inside and I do feel that I do not have to face anyone or anything in here but, I do not feel cut off from the world either as I can hear everything that I want to hear and do only what I want to. It is my only safe haven.

My ears carry on ignoring the chitter chatter of the idle talker even though I can see their thin lips making different moves of expression and my nose can smell the varied food smells of the breakfast foods and my head can sense the outsiders all standing like little soldiers waiting patiently to be fed. They must be so happy that at least someone has died and they get fed for free. On one side there is grief and on the other side there is joy. If they were ever asked about why they were here today, they would say "death" has brought them here but may not even have a clue about who exactly has died and yet, if asked, what they had eaten here, they would be able to count and tell.

I fell in and out of sleep and I amazed myself as I really do not know how I can sleep for such a long time, but then I am not fast asleep continuously. I am thinking it is me time. My head feels clear and calm in here and I know that Kaka has been with the breakfast plate and the hot tea and he has left without me replying to his beckoning. A couple of females have been in urging me to get up, eat and get dressed appropriately and show my face downstairs. No one gets a reply and none of them check to see if I am dead or alive. No one leave a trail of their smell so I cannot identify who they are. I do not need to eat in here. I am neither moving nor using energy so I do not need to eat.

Lunch time has come and gone and I can hear the scurry of people wiping the dusty floor and their marked mouths as they walk to and fro with their stained clothes and the ladies coming upstairs to use the toilet and flushing the loo in amazement. It is a novelty for some of them as quite a few people still wash the filth down with water in their old toilets. The wealthy or well to do people have the English style up right sitting position toilets rather than the squatting ones. I can see them using the squiggly golden luscious hand wash. They stand hovering over the bottle like the vampire over prey and as they run their dry crinkly over worked cold hands under the free flowing hot water, that's a luxury and then they caress their hands over their necks and cheeks to lessen the murkiness of the days sweat.

After lunchtime, Father popped in but there was no response from me, even though he sat on my bed, touched and soothed me with his fat warm hands and he strokes my legs to wake me up. I can feel and sense him in every which way, the father trying to get through to me and the wise man trying to mellow the burning inside of me with his old wisdom. No one is listening here and my heart is too cold to feel his warmth. I can sense myself carrying on and so does everyone else as they have done their duty and so they must be off now and I continue with my pains. Through the whiskers of the tiger and deep within the warmth of his fur I could sense the night drawing in almost as if my shutters were closed against the curtains of my eyes. I open my eyes wide and I can see small flickers of darkness against my long lashes and I could see her coming towards me. I take the blanket off and look towards the bedroom door, it is still open wide, suddenly my eyes wonder towards the window, the dark grey clouds were definitely coming for me and yet I know there's no cloud in the sky outside, abruptly I jump out of bed as my spine shudders and I know that the place I am in, is not good so I leave her shaded darkness behind me.

I did not know where I was heading to, but first of all I went to the bathroom where I started to admire the girls face in the clear white mirror in front of me. She did look an awful lot like me and I know that I looked just the way that I have looked all those other days and yet, I couldn't relate to what I was looking at. Nothing has had any effect on me and that is certainly good and anyhow, no one dragged me to go and put my thumb print on that ballot paper that has only one name on it and there I was, thinking that I would be able to choose who I vote for. I don't think I vote any way. I wouldn't be allowed.

With my index finger I firmly rub my front two teeth, they squeak and I smile because that means that they are clean so, I do not need to brush them. I may just check before I really go to sleep for the night as sleeping during the daytime definitely plays with my mind. There are no visible lines of pain on her face but I can see my own cracks bluntly like the pencil which has not yet been scraped through the sharp side of life. Once again the girl in the mirror shows her big smiling teeth as

I politely smile back at her, there seems to be no darkened pain within her, but I do not know about that myself as her eyes look tired and soar and I can see a shade of dark skin under her eyes. Maybe she should sleep more as I have done today but then, I know I have not slept properly in days and I still look fine. I look down at her tummy and I can see a small ripple of ribs, perhaps she should eat a bit more. Maybe she is a bit like me!

"Meera, what are you doing?" shouted father as he carefully paraded his eyes around his bedroom. The floor was full of Mother's clothes and her shoe wardrobe was fully ajar where my eyes could meet the matching of the clothes to the shoes. Each suit and sari was perfectly pressed and the shawls, warm and tender and the veils colourful and in full bloom. "I thought you were still in bed resting or in your room. Anyhow, when did you come in here and what is all this, dear Mimi?"

"Well papa, it's getting dark in here and outside," I said.

He was not listening to my words but was watching me thumping my heart gently and then, once again there was silence. "Well at least you are up girl, so let's eat dinner together once more." This time I didn't ignore him but I searched for that something that would touch that shade of dark grey inside and I didn't want it to stain a dark purple colour. Bruises I don't like and they cause pain inside and leave a mark on the outside. I see that purple colour and I touch the colour purple and I slowly put my cold hand on to his warm

118

hand, he quietly clenches it tightly and it feels so soothing and calming. He pulls me up to rise with him and we both stood still and tall listening to the silence and her echoes and then he gently led me as I followed. I see a glimpse of that girl in the big mirror with the even bigger smile. Something has made her happy tonight.

Father, Kaka and I all sit as we did last night and I do not scratch the corners of my hot plate or rub the fork across the food or even smear the juices, instead I sit comfortably and wait. When we were ready I quickly say out loud a prayer that Mama used to recite and it was time consuming and I quivered on and on and even that was fine as somehow it all brought a bit of her to us. Some knew these rituals like the back of their hands where as others have to quiver in our soggy boots to string a few bits together. The chanting of good food, good people, the good world and health and the absence of all those who have found better places away from this bad world of red blood and the blue ink on the outside peoples thumbs and the print of the red and blue inks and I can see their lips quickly saying "Amen". That was a queue for me to shut up! Sitting and eating at this grand dining table was so real and so much a part of our everyday life and right now, it felt as if nothing had changed. That little thing hope, had crept up from within. I need hope now.

We ate, drank but couldn't be merry and so instead, we all listened to the radio and not the news, but to melodious songs of different genre and within those were the ones that Kaka whistled to. somehow these songs brought a piece of 'home' to us whilst we sipped coffee and licked the sugars from the corners of our mouths and wiped dry the white cream left behind from the delight in our mouth and then the far cry of the echoes of the yawns followed. I went straight to my bedroom where tiger was waiting with great abundance and as I looked into the mirror, she looked as if she had seen better days. Tonight was just another night where I jumped face down on to my bed and the bare feet were dirty and I could feel the dirt between my toes and bits of food in between my fingers nails but then tiger couldn't really see me. I pulled him or her up and over my head. He was smothering me once more, tiger love never felt so huggingly good.

A few days had gone by and really I only noticed the days slowly wishing themselves away when I was once again, in front of the mirror as I scratched my front two teeth and a whole load of nasty surprise came off. I convinced myself that the next time she looks back at me she will have both her two front teeth missing. I picked up the toothbrush and squidged some stripy toothpaste across it and scrubbed it all over my teeth. As if any idiot really has a clue about keeping things safe. Surprisingly enough as my tongue licked my lips it felt as if all was really clean and tingling fresh. A few days had gone by but how come I never realised how many days had actually gone by and what I had done with life. Forgotten days and forgotten people. I look at the tall ceiling but it didn't have any inscriptions of past people, but I did remember myself standing in front of this mirror, many a times and then in a flicker of an eyelid and without even rinsing my mouth, I fled quietly into my bedroom and frantically rummaged through the pages of the empty calendar where days and dates didn't match up. It was a Rubik cube and I had to try and sort it to match the numbers to the days and months. The harder I tried to remember the day and the date, the more my tongue got twisted as if I was two people living in one body and a part of my own brain was dead and yet I was so very much alive.

I started at the beginning of May, it could not be the first or second, a third, fourth fifth or sixth because..... I did not know why or how I knew that but I did and then, I could not remember what happened on any of those days, but I was definitely sure that I had lived that week so then, I moved my fingers onto the number lucky seven and then slowly slid my finger on eight, nine, ten and wonderful heaven eleven. Eleven, twelve and unlucky thirteen and my fourteenth birthday when we all went to Malaysia for a holiday. I remember that and why my finger would not move off that, I don't know. Fifteen, sweet sixteen and then straight onto the end of the May and so I did that again and again, from fifteen to sixteen to the end of the month.

Why, oh why is it that I cannot recall any of the in between days? Why is it I don't remember and where was I for all these forgotten days and why I cannot remember? Remember, remember Meera, try to remember kid, I know I am only a kid and I am glad that I am just a stupid kid who has lost sight of days and life lived within those days. Time, yes I know the time. Time heals and I know that big Ben is still in the massive hall where it's always been so I run frantically to see it again and I will see it just as it is, for the light never goes off in front of his eyes. From the calendar to the hall I peer straight into Bens eyes. Its big hand is rushing quickly to the twelve whilst the small hand lazily sleeps on the eleven or is it one. Eleven o'clock in the night. What day is it then, Meera?! Forget the day, I should be in bed now but what night is this? My eyes are full of sleep and my head full of questions but all the other lights are out, which means only one thing, sleep time.

All night long I dozed in and out of sleep and the only thing that my mind questioned my being was the day and I waited for the new dawn to crack so that, it may bring with it some new memories and if all fails, then I could ask someone. I did not feel her warmth or the tigers warmth and the restless thing inside of me meant that I was eager to get my answers to come out of the closet and as I look straight at myself, I realize that I only remember myself in these fully worn clothes. Day and night clothes, that is strange. I run out of my bedroom and I can see a glimpse of natural light and in silence, I go and sit in that armchair in the sitting room. I do feel like going to the toilet but right now even that will need to wait. I need to know the day and right now, right here, that is the most important thing and yet I sit and wonder what time Kaka will get up. I keep my legs crossed firmly and I have become a bit anxious so I cross my arms as well, as if I am crossed with so many words. I twitch and scratch and ache and as I scratch my head as if it were dirty and I can see the dirty hands and feet and I continue till I am feeling sore and red.

The World Service radio is sitting in front of me and hums away as if it is snoring lightly with its melody but that's not the burning question right now, nor is the elections or even the reds and blues, but I see the glimpse of the golden brown knob and run my slimy dirty fingers and in an instant I realize that the room has lit up with the voices of the presenter coming out of the metal box. It's a man as always and he's going on and on and I can hear the voice without actually hearing the words and the woman in the background trying to say something, unfelt and unheard. I am thinking long and hard and then there are empty pennies that have clicked into some sort of a slot, and suddenly without a warning the penny finally drops.

"It is nearly six o'clock and let us catch up with the news from around the world followed by a round-up of what's happening here in Incredible India." My head tightly focused on six o'clock and unwittingly I found myself repeating that on and on until. "It is the twenty-eighth of May and the time is a few seconds away from six o'clock and what a scorcher it is going to be today but for now, it is time for the news." Six o'clock and the twenty-eighth, six o'clock and the twenty-eighth, six o'clock and, and.... and.... the twenty-eighth. This date and time kept ringing again and again and then I found myself running up the stairs and in the background, I can still hear the news and the memory of his rugged chewed up face even though, I have never seen these faces but they have to be miserable people because they give out messages of misery. Suddenly all that had become a faded memory. I rushed and my flustered steps carried my legs until I reached the mouth of my bedroom and placed my finger on the 28th on the calendar. My eyes searched frantically for a pen out of my school bag that might help me mark the day or date, but that would mean that I would need to take my finger off the calendar and just as I had found a day or date, I couldn't possibly take my finger off what I had found.

The dresser next to me has eyeliner on it which I have bought but never used, that worked really well on the paper calendar as I carefully drew a big bold thick circle around that number. I put a ring around that confusing number fifteen. I count the days between fifteen all the way to twenty eight and somehow in my own head it doesn't add up, so I then use my fingers, which did actually make sense. Fifteen to sixteen on my left thumb, sixteen to seventeen on my next finger and the fat one in the middle is seventeen to eighteen. Twenty on one hand, twenty five on the other hand and then the right hand again and the fat middle finger once again makes number twenty eight and that makes thirteen days altogether, that's it, where have these thirteen days gone?

Unlucky thirteen. I go straight into the bathroom and there on the rail is my bathroom robe and towel. I grab the head and shoulders shampoo and the dove shower gel from the rack and step into the tray and then throw my clothes out and shut the glass sliding door and yet I have not shut the bathroom door itself! But hey, I know that no one ever comes to my bathroom anyway! Father has his own en suite and Kaka has his own down stairs. I can feel the sizzling steam all around me and I could feel my hair sizzling from the roots and I could no longer tell if it was the condensation or the heat within me and yet my body feels dry within. There are no tears and no fluttering discomfort or even the uneasy lips quivering away or the nose that widens with anger under the heated misted sensation and there is serene calmness. I wash away the missing days and the sleepless nights and the disputed events and then there's the winner and others who are always the losers. Winners and losers and I am nowadays always the loser and I know, that some are born winners like the politicians and then there are always the losers like the ones outside and a bit like me. No one is a winner, not really.

A long hot shower, cleansing of the body and soul and then a changing of the clothes, hair combed all back till all the kicks and flicks are erased and tamed and then smothered with luscious dove cream to soothe the cares away and in the head a new search for the perfect sandals whilst walking on the beach. All of this therapy can be found in Mother's bedroom, its haven, and now I am the keeper and owner of all of it. I hiss happily against her dressing table and I can clearly see the perfumes, lotions and potions and without even looking at it and I didn't want to look because I don't want to be tempted or rewarded by all these goodies and against my wishes and better judgment. I do need a piece of her and this may be the nearest thing possible for now at least. The things here and in her wardrobes are the connections between the two people and this room has to bring that kid into being a woman and maybe these will help.

The long thin liquid eye-liner stretches from the inner to the outer edge of my eye as the long thick sleek top and bottom makes its mark and the rustic and dusky plum colours are dabbed on the high cheek bones with a whisky brush and finally the damson lipstick, thick and formed, presses against the thick lips into shape. A mini version of the mother I don't have but I do have me and I will take a little of her with me all the while. The final touch of perfumed spray and it has that uplifting sensation and carefully I out the woman into place by gathering the veil slowly onto my head. Half-covered half-not and I feel complete as all the pieces of the jigsaw have gone into place. A complete manipulation of the girl into a woman.

It was just as well that Father had already gone downstairs as what would I have done and said to father, would there have been frowns or disapproving smirking on the face and what will Kaka actually say, I know they would not approve but then, this isn't for them. Does this mean that I would have to come into this room to make myself into a woman and so the girl can stay in her room but the transformation of the woman has to take place in here? In a reluctant manner, I hastily tread down the grand stairs away from my own room and I see her looking at me in a disproving manner and I question her under my breath, as to why it is good for her but not for me. Elsewhere, no one is looking, as I elegantly walk with a hint of confidence and I don't want to lose that little that I do actually have. My left hand is swinging by my side whilst the right held, just at the corner of the chin shading my cheek and a bit of the bright eye fully woken as she walked. I strode passed the kitchen and its owner and as he distracted himself but I chose to ignore and yet I heard the cry, is it you Rani Madam? Alarm bells rang within his tone.

My feet froze and the left finger dangled by my side as it stayed perfectly silent as Kaka quickly rushed to the kitchen door to take a glimpse of me himself. He did not utter a word but I could imagine his eyes widen further and further and then, I kept that stare onto the blank pale wall in front of me. Father came out of the diner whilst scratching his head at what he heard and then in utter amazement, his jaw dropped. His teeth were still as if he had sucked on an ice cube, his tongue, a dark shade of pink resting neatly between his teeth and empty mouth. His brow arched in disgust and sheer shock but more with a confused glare so white and cold and the trembling voice uttered "Mimi dearest Mimi, what is all this dressing up all in aid of? You don't have to grow into her shoes or even grow up just yet and why are you copying her, it's totally uncalled for?"

Now, my own face showed disappointment as his words rung in my ears again and again and as he stood still watching. He could tell that I always cried silent tears but for the first time in ages, he could hear me weep but it was full of pain. Pain that no plaster or germoline cream can erase or even kiss better or even numb with antiseptic. His tone had afflicted this pain by scolding me. He gently shortened the gap between me and him by putting his hand over my shoulders and calming my turmoil and all the while, edging me to go inside. We took our seats at the table and watched one another in despair and yet no words matched or uttered what we both had felt. It is strange how silence can scratch and the mark the hidden pain and still there is no sigh of relief.

We had breakfast together like a family, almost like a normal family now and what's normal and yet there was this eerie silence on the walls, but if you didn't listen carefully enough, then you wouldn't even hear it or notice its effect and on the surface, it all looks so perfectly calm and cool and you can hear the knocking of the unsung wind. After breakfast, the plates were moved into the kitchen, table sprayed horizontally over and cloth wiped across vertically, air freshener sprayed into the air as always and then, the lingering aroma of soft sandal wood sticks lit and then, breakfast became an almost distant memory. The paperboy had flung today's words over the big gate, the milkman had left the white froth wrapped in a thick clear plastic bag and the Rusk boys shouting with their tantalizing voices in a sure hope of selling something today. The burning desire to put a penny in his pocket, but of course not here in our house as no one really liked this desire much and we only got some to keep for the odd visitor. All the boys had been and the men as well and Kaka had gone walkabouts doing his normal duties, except for one thing and that is that he was still not singing yet. His whistling had lost its wind around the house. On the surface normality had sparked but inside, the story of the empty walls told different tales of the forgotten ghosts.

"Kaka, are you not singing like you normally would be?" I found it hard to make this ushered normal conversation. He stopped his chores but continued looking on the floor where each tile joins its corner from one to the next as Kaka looks attentively at the dirt in between them. That is what I saw as I looked at his narrowing eyes, and perhaps he saw the pain imbedded between himself and us and these tiles. Quickly I wipe the tears away with my sleeve before he could see as I move to turn the radio on and his songs were on and his face lit up. He looked on like a shy child who had been rewarded with a lollipop but with a guilty pleasure of knowing that he should not be craving it. I smiled at him but his face looked embarrassed or probably guilty for being happy. It didn't seem ok to be happy or normal or just carrying on with life but he knew what I had said as he nodded and shied away. We moved around the house from one corner to the other, pretending to be happy and to be busy doing nothing really worthwhile. I listened to every move of ours and I heard Father humming to the sound of the music and memories.

"Papa did you win or lose the election?" I asked, something that he was not expecting me to ask or be concerned about, but kindly putting his hands on the base of the arm chair and looking with a thoughtful mind, his shoulders broadened and a big minty sigh of relief smoothly breathed out. "You lost your seat in the election didn't you Father, that's why your mates don't come anymore?"

"No dearest Meera, I have lost all in life, my wife and our family unit, as for my seat it doesn't feel like a win at all. I have lost the most important thing in life itself and as for friends, they are neither here or there and we need time to grieve as a family, together." I went on and asked about the election fever and why it didn't take place after the elections as we have seen in the past and he gently replied that if one looks eagerly and attentively they will see the election fever all around them most of the time. I carried on by saying that normally there is a lot of song and dance and free flowing of food and drink and people running wild in the streets and houses, having chanting processions late in the night, to which he replied that maybe I didn't have the ears to hear all that and nor the eyes to see all the commotion, because all of this did happen, but just not here. The only thing that actually felt quite alive was the vibrant colours of her clothes and the more that I looked, the more she was alive and really the only live memory were her belongings. Her body belonged within these fabrics and the silky garments and gold threaded sandals with the frilly lace garments. All of these were like the royal belongings and then there was her make-up and extravagant jewellery. Make-up I could use to mascarade her but the jewellery was priceless.

From that day onward, the ice had been broken and the cracks had make their mark and we tried to put the past where it belonged, within us rather than on the surface. The surface that had her remains in, that beautiful urn a gorgeous golden vase sitting prettily on the mantel piece and father said that we would one day, together, find her final resting place. Somewhere like a long river which has no mouth or edge and she always liked the freedom of a flying dove. Doves fly but don't often rest. Maybe she needs sanity and so a flower bed with the bright blue sky above, may be the right place as it will be quite, a bit like her and as for the river and its vibrancy and the people who adorn its flow and she will be amongst the living of young and old alike. Water has many uses, ducks, cattle and humans all dipping their pretty feet and the child who has water thrown on its head to mould it into something and the ritual cleansing with water and its healing properties. Maybe she should be in water after all. Maybe I should also visit a river to find harmony who ever she is and it is a she for definite, her inside and me and on the outside of the river, sitting there with my back to life. The more I thought about it the more it was dragging me to it. The force of the howling water was calling me.

Breakfast was the same now as ever before with the dark wood seeing us three seated on its verge and clanging of the dishes and scratching of cutlery and father resting his belly so that the food could merrily go down and Kaka and I filtering into the deep air around the heavy house, trying to look and feel busy as words were not freely forth coming and something had to be going on. Lunchtimes were dominant as the set time had been deactivated and evening meals were actually enjoyable and for the first time in a long time we all three had our meals together. In between meals, Father was in and out of the house and Kaka's feet never stood still and neither did his mouth very much. A few weeks had dragged by and Father's friends had moved back in to our lives which made our closed environment a bit more normal. Normal was like going to school but I don't know why but it was as if I had been robbed of the child years because, I simply was not a child any longer and I had to look after the two men as I was the only female in this house now.

That day I changed myself so that I could do exactly that and so I went and took off the clothes that the young girl always wore, plain and simple and instead, today I wore her sari for the first time. I carefully with love, draped it around me and it felt as if it was actually made just for me and then, I added the finishing touch. I placed the veil of the sari over three-quarters of the way on to my head, that's how she did it also. Without hesitating I slipped my feet into her sandals and strapped myself into them whilst the little girl kicked her flip flops from next, loosely under the bed. The woman stood at the dresser and plastered on her face cream and then, with precision, she plastered the walls of her face and coated the outer corners of the wide smile and not knowing what to do with the misted perfumed spray, she pressed the button and watched it fizz into the heavy air. She smiled, carefully strode out of the room and walked towards them as they looked and gasped with so many questions in their minds. All I heard was the baffled words strung into short verses but for me, all I could think of was, the fact that mother and daughter or girl and woman had rolled into one without noticing or thinking. I had found home.

Chapter 6

Consequences, we do not think of and nor do we know what the future holds for us, but I was about to find out soon enough. Soon enough the days had gotten shorter. It was getting dark at around six and the mornings and evenings were cold and even during the day, there was a tingle of cold reaching our spines. We closed our windows much earlier and opened them much later and then, when the outside was shut out, the heating would purr along like the silent cat and it would become cozy, warm, dusky and comfortable and yet, the days were always bright, sunny and somewhat chilly. It was November now and life's days were just rolling by but nothing was happening, so I thought.

I remember how the spooky neighbourhood children with their Halloween, tricks or treats, came out in the dark. "Guy Fawkes" was blown up and of course "bonfire night" was celebrated with fireworks by the Christians in our own community, whilst all the other religions watched on and enjoyed all the excitement, even though most of us did not even know what these celebrations were all about. It was a time for a little bit of happiness. The explosion of the fireworks caused sparks within us and even that little bit felt good. We all know what Christmas was about and yet our own celebration of Diwali was almost like a normal day in nautical

November this year. We lit the lamps. We cooked a bit extra and we watched the outside world having fun from inside. We were on the inside but wanted so dearly to be on the outside on this day. We were not in a mood to celebrate life but somehow that spark of hope was ignited even now, but maybe it was just too soon for some things.

Putting Diwali aside whilst blowing out the lamps that brightened up people's lives, we moved on to a normal day in this big house where three people lived together yet living almost separate lives. Diligent December had crept up soon enough and some of the locals had started to put the decorations up. From Father's bedroom window, I looked on at the joy of Father Xmas shining brightly with his reindeers. It was always such a joy when we watched them and they watched our divine Diwali lights but it was not a competition. Soon enough Christian women would wrap their heads in scarfs with their longer than knee-length dresses and flip-flops underneath and a Kashmir warm, cozy shawl around their shoulders, heading off for their Midnight Mass and the clanging of the church bells creating a beautiful symphony of sound to our mystical and somewhat musical ears and I did not even know what they did at Midnight Mass but I was excited nevertheless. The word "Mass" sounds huge.

Crowning and glorious Christmas Day and as I sat and looked out of that very same window, today I was in the same position but looking at the Christmas cheer, little girls with pig-tails and princess dresses and boys with the side-parting on their sleek straight hair and mothers and fathers holding each other hands, looking like real families wearing their best happy smiles that had been taken out after a year. There must be colourful wrapping paper with exciting presents under their brightly-lit trees and the turkey and lamb legs in the hot glowing oven purring in their own juices, with the brown fluffy potatoes sitting beside the meat, sizzling alongside the parsnips and sprouts. Festive food may be the real reason why they have the big smiles on their lips first thing in the morning. After church, mothers huddle themselves into the kitchen to stir the thick juicy gravy and Father's start the Christmas party with brandy flames.

A family gathering together and ours will never be. Such is life. I can hear Father's friends stirring in the living room downstairs and their cold coughs through their mufflers as I watch and they enter our big gate. I can hear Kaka swapping the utensils around in the kitchen and a maid is taking charge of the main meal. The smells roam all around the house and it should feel comforting but it doesn't anymore, the way it used to. I go downstairs led by the aroma of the curries being made and as I stand near the kitchen, I wonder why so much is being cooked today and as I reflect, I can see that there are prayer plates out with varieties of food and drinks and men sitting with Father, smoking and getting ready for prayers, parading around the big table that has been opened and there laid the big clean white tablecloth and all the shiny cutlery buffed to the shine just like freshly brushed Colgate clean teeth.

"Meera, dear, come inside."

"No Father, come out."

Father quickly came out and looked straight into my eyes. He took my hands into his big hands and gently whispers into my ears, "Meera, dearest, the young Councilor sitting at the head of the table is a good man and I have just given your hand in marriage and now we are going to do the ceremonial prayer, so cover your head and come and sit at the other end of the table."

Like an obedient girl who is told to sit at the table to eat breakfast even though the person inside does not want to eat, I take my seat. I sit, as my father then helps me to push the chair into a comfortable position but my feet do not feel comforted even though I am wearing Mother's shoes as always now. I lay them gently flat onto the rug that sleeps quietly underneath this heavy wooden table. My hands clasp each other gently and I can feel the sweat warming them up as they lay sweetly in my lap. My back that is against the firmness of the back rest is being gently stirred, but the insides are truthfully shaken. My cold feet and yet I know they are warm huddle as I sit here, it is hard to know or understand what exactly I am doing here.

I have been asked to come in and take a seat in my own house and yet in front of all these people, or rather men, who I have never noticed before and it is not customary for us women to look at the male visitors unless they have come with their wives or children. Today it seems as if everything, including this "not such a bad life after Mother" was an alien life to me, as if all of a sudden it is not mine anymore. It is still Christmas Day and I could assume that they are all here to have a Christmas drink with Father and whenever the door is shut, that is what they do, smoke and drink. It is a "male-only" zone then and even though Kaka went in and out of that room, Mother and I hardly ever did.

The longer that the cracks of the door are closed to us women, the louder the voices of the wild boars got and there would be bursts of thunderous claps and some taunting sniggering remarks, of trials and tribulations and all the while, I peered through the main crack, the smells of the fragrant strong masculine cigars and cigarette smoke smoldering and the slow tinkering of the expensive crystal glasses and dark bottles smooched one another. The following morning, I would always race to see this room and the remainder of the happy night before.

I listen to the clattering of the cluttered cutlery, the plates warmed and the glasses shined, all like marching soldiers in a neat line on this big table and then each glass placemat acts as a coaster for the plate and on the sides, the decorated cutlery is placed with the napkins twirled together into the glasses. How great it all looks but it is not a great occasion. Quietly, without others looking up at me, I feel the plate. It is still warm, unlike how I feel inside. My Father goes to smell the food that is laid, side-by-side, and at the corner of his mouth, I can see his dribble with the aromatic smells of the foods laid out.

He starts to mutter about how he has given my hand in marriage to the guy who sat opposite me and yet the election fever now brought this man to me and into my life. How can this be? He sits opposite me but I have never seen him and refuse to look at him. Father's words Councillor and elected rubbish and his life revolving around the elections and the turmoil it has on our life now and on my mother's life and now it has entered my life once again. I was thinking that now they have left us for good, rid of grief, but the election fever has come back to stay. Father said he has lost but there are all his friends and why is he convinced that I am going to say "yes" to his "mate"?

I sit and think back and I can hear how the food is served up and everyone is eating. Dessert has also been dished up and then the coffees have been placed close to each ten individual places and on one side from the corner of my eye, I can see Father and Kaka sitting and then the rest are all eating and slurping more than they should. I can hear Kaka saying that I have not touched my food or drank anything. The election fever has come to haunt me and all I can think about it, that the election took my mother away and now just as it was peaceful, it has come back to haunt me once again and somehow, I feel isolated and very alone now. Father and his mates, Kaka and the house, and me and the dead.

Father takes my hand and I can see a ring almost as nasty as a Coke can ring coming towards me like a snooze. Father tells me to put my hand forward a little more so that the ring could be put onto it by him. "I'll take that, thanks!" and with that, I get up and I shoot out of the room straight into my bedroom. The metal snooze is in my palm and I can still hear his final words ringing in my ears, "Don't worry councilor, she is shy, don't worry." I was not a shy girl and so he is feeding these people with lies and it is not right and he has fed me something that is never going to be digested. I put the metal snooze on my dresser and I get on with my life. I tidy my room and then go into Father's room and tidy her clothes and I line up his socks like soldiers even though they were already tidy. She didn't like mess and I still want to please her, but I leave my wondering in the corner where he always leaves his clothes, piled up for someone else to tidy up.

Back in my room, I sit on my bed and think about what I do not know. It is strange and creepy that I feel almost in a daze, a little confused and fidgety and I just cannot put my finger on what exactly. I sit till my head and body drops and I no longer can sit anymore. I pull the duvet over my head and leave the lion blanket back. The duvet feels suffocating and I enjoy its burden, the heaviness and warmth and yet I can smell my own smell from it, almost of other's dirty hair and not

140

mine. That cannot be my own smell, I know that. I put that to the back of my mind and focus on what is happening to me and my life, but in front of me, I can see both of my parents. Why is he doing this to me, this metal snooze is going to be a part of me forever. A placement of her. I deserve it.

My left thumb has this awkward itchy feeling whenever I am not relaxed and over the past six months at least, it has become quite a norm. I am fed up of hearing my own crying and the gentle tears draining my eyes as I lay like a helpless child under this thick covering. I scratch my thumb but it causes me stress so it doesn't relieve anything. I try to rub it but the sensation is in need of a lot more so, I just leave it to throb, just like me. We are both alike, both cannot survive without the other and yet we can offer no hope either. Maybe I could get it cut off and then there will be no agitation at all, my life may be smooth just like the thumb but then others who will look at it, may mock and taunt me, but at least that would be better than the affliction of pain within. I am sure that I can hear myself falling off to sleep but the echoes of my tear droplets from the nose onto the pillow leave a louder lull fall and then, they disperse like a soluble aspirin reaching those inner parts. The tighter I close my eyes, the more the room moves around me and somehow this concussion feels comforting as it dulls the whacking pains within my brain cells somewhere. The sweet aching in my heart and the turbulence in my head along with the dried out eye sockets are all good medicinal things to put one off to sleep. But tomorrow is another day.

The next day I was in my routine once again and with the reminder of the Coke can ring, stirred but not fizzy. Father was downstairs and quickly I thought I would go and have breakfast with him as I could smell the food and the gentle radio humming away like a sweet bird in the background and the subtle humming of the two males singing along. We all have our breakfast together and do the little chores together and then a new girl who has started coming to clean and help with bits of cooking rings the gate buzzer as I look on from Mother's bedroom. I spend all morning still in my old clothes just watching out of the window. She sat here that "election fever" night and it is almost as if the fever has never left us, but she has.

Father comes and goes and I can hear the sweeping brush with its wooden handle being scraped slowly along by her. Her. No that is not good, she told me her name that first day when I called her "You" and she so assertively told me that she is not "You" but "Maria". Tiny little thing that moves like the wild wind, fast and furious and yet she is quite nice. Once she finishes the cleaning, she makes her favourite English tea and watches the television until lunchtime. She scurries herself along and happily gets on with the lunch and tidying up, washing, wiping and the big red smile wide as ever, happily taking her happy life in her stride. Around six o'clock, she waves everyone a big goodbye with both hands together and in a flash, she would be gone, shame she doesn't use it on the surface. She spoke English brilliantly but she didn't go to my English school that I used to go to over half a year ago. She was a Christian girl so she didn't need to go to an English school that was for Indian children. She was in a league of her own.

As I watched her leave and still waving, I saw father closing the gate behind her and then he saw me staring out of his window. He stood still and silent and kept watching me with a kind smile and then he lifted his left hand and lapped the fingers with the right hand. I shouted back "OK, I will put the Coke can ring on," and with that his eyes smiled a little wider and with a gentle squint. He was a good man deep down inside, he really was, maybe not transparent at times and misunderstood often. Whilst my head was wondering in the direction of the Coke can ring, I saw his friends coming in from the big gate. He wasn't just seeing Maria out, but waiting for the election fever men. I ran to the dressing table and started searching for it. I know I put it here last night. If I do not find it, Father will think I have lost it deliberately and I do not want to disappoint him.

I searched for over an hour all over the room. I even went through his pockets and even though Mother only had a few pockets, I even searched through them and her jewellery boxes and then it clicked that how would I have found it here? I had put it on my own dressing table, not Mother's. The dresser had become mine and it was my second room, almost mine but here, everything was civilized and not panicky. It was all straight and still, a bit lifeless and in ruin, it was a bit of havoc in mine. I could hear the rumbling voices of the election friends and even though I could not see them, I could sense them sitting with their hands pressing their black moustaches and rubbing their lips so tightly with their fingers and trying not to sit like perfect gentlemen by sitting with their legs wide-open and their clean, freshly soap-washed bodies, in their crispy clean starched-ironed clothes and their hands and faces always smelling of soap, maybe Dove soap. I use that too.

Once in my own room, I hunted high and low for that Coke can ring and I remembered where I had left it. I had thrown it into the little bin next to my bed. As I lay in my bed, I could see it sparkling. I took it and placed it on my finger. It fitted perfectly on my middle finger and then I went to show my face downstairs. I stood against the crack where they were all sitting and as I listened on to what they were saying, none of the election jargon made any sense. It left me wondering if that was all life was for Father. Some were vultures and others were the prey.

So I headed off to the kitchen and stood beside Kaka. He was serving food and talked even though he was extremely busy but he talked and I listened, not to him but to the sound of the house. It was as it used to be all that time ago. That was normal then and now. The sound of the pin dropping could still be heard against the gently perfect compositions of music on the radio and then, there is the obedient Kaka and almost the Master of this house and yet, he never will be "the Master" and then there is a female without a place or position in life let alone in this house.

Christmas was a great festival to take my mind off our life and there was still New Year's Eve and the New Year's Day parties when some people who need an excuse to get happy, will drink themselves to that convincing silly state. I think it is a figment of their imagination, but it is a good place to be, forgetting about the world and us. The week gap between Christmas and New Year's Day slowly drifted along and Father shared drinks and conversations with his mates behind the closed doors and I silently sat on my mother's seat and watched the celebration go by from the silent window. There was no noise of the elections or the sightings of the winners or the domination of the losers outside and my stupidity and that fact that I was a mere naïve child, meant that the elections, the winners and losers, were all gathered here under this roof.

New Year's Eve saw Kaka, Father and myself busily along with the help of a few working ladies preparing canapés, drinks and lots of banqueting snacks. The door that lit open the big room was pushed aside and the wooden table extended out gifts of food for everyone. Father simply explained that just because Mother was no longer alive that does not mean that all traditions should be sealed away into an empty envelope, in fact quite the opposite, as she always loved the noise of the house guests, to which I quietly added that her desire was just to please Father, that was all. Even though my comment had a lot of burdened weight, it was almost as if I had not even spoken as my thoughts pondered because, wherever my steps stood still, it was as if she had treaded on that exact spot last year and as I opened my nostrils to enjoy her absence in person, deep down inside, she was very much still alive and here within this room. It was worth carrying on.

Father had told us of the colour theme, being red again this year but unlike last year, it was just red without the black or white tarnishing it. It was supposed to be perfect but in fact it was far from it. It was colourful without being spoilt, red like Father Xmas with the runny nose like strawberries oozing out the juices or her lying with the red lips and the red blood slowly dripping into the cold life, all far from being perfect. Red clothes and red veil covered half of my head as I ripped the bud of the cloth tightly with a hairpin, lots of red cloth hugged my body. The hard wooden table is softened by the luscious varnish and a slow burden of red cloth covers it. I stare at it for ages and then at my own. There are no real choices.

Soon enough, the cocktail sticks prick the stem and steady plates, the drinks flow from glasses to licking lips and the nibbles pass from the trays to the every-ready fingers. I stand in the center of the room and steadily keep turning around to observe the laughing of wide mouths and the moustached men, twitching delightfully at the corners of their mouths and the lips movement continuously at the continuous words of delight. The election fever had delightfully come into our house and even though I had spent most of my life seeing it, I can remember hating it also. Somehow today it felt good. There wasn't a moment where I had time to think about real life and yet this was it. Overflowing talk of the elected, the losers campaigning in a quest to put their point and bribe across and the champions who have the winning goal. I should have felt uncomfortable within a room of over thirty men, but I had not been here before and I didn't want it to end because I belonged in this house and I was a part of it myself. Maybe I could talk to the men and pretend to be just like them. I see that guy who gave me that Coke can ring a few days ago. Quickly, I look at my hands. It isn't where it should be. "Should" is a respected man's word.

It is half past eleven and it is still New Year's Eve and I am still standing where I was before except now I have been to my bedroom and found that thing that pays the price for respect and hurriedly after hunting it down, it is on my finger, left hand, third finger and no one in this room has even noticed the respect on me, nor the fact that I was even in the room. No one dared to talk to me because, my father was in here and I know, that if Father was out of the equation, these men were thick and slimy. Big fat bodies with thick fat sweaty hands. Quietly, I hold my hands out in front of me and I feel a slow widening of my lips. My hands are not like theirs but, I do want to be like them.

I started to ask him inquisitive questions, his name, where he lives, what he did for work and most of all, why he chose to give me that Coke can ring. The Coke can ring was decided by the parents and he worked with his father as both are elected councillors. As a local resident, he knows Father quite well and his name, so hard to pronounce, so Noddy was his nickname. His father ruled their house I could tell, and he was the puppy that followed. He was on the leash and jumped when daddy dearest told him to do so. I know someone else like that as well. This marriage could actually work. We have certain things in common. Yes, I should marry him and "should" is important.

He laughed like the rest and spoke the same elected language and I too know this, so we had this amazing conversation like a kid to candy. Our conversation took place often and he became a real friend indeed, someone who I shared everything with and told my inner demons to without him ever judging me. We had become friends but not friendly enough to be married. We didn't disagree and yet we were not close enough to even hold hands and our friendship was almost like two same-sex friends, not best friends, just good friends. A lot in common. It felt as if that Coke can ring had twisted us together. New Year's Eve went into the night, secrets and problems shared, new beginnings making an entry without even knowing, just like the new day. It was so late and as the men were winding down, I was out of it, eyes drooping with heavy sleep bags, mouth unable to open anymore because of the amount of talking it did with that one person only and I am sure, that his ears must have deafened with all the words that I spilled out. And then, without a thought, I found myself in my bed and I did not even have time to think of how I got there and with whom, but I was glad I was there.

The room laid silent and yet bursting with crispy sunshine as I slowly opened my eyes and looked at the striking electric clock on my bedside draw. It was eleven o'something, "eleven!" By the time that eleven approached we were thinking more about lunchtime and yet how could I still be in bed? I poked my ear out of the duvet but no sounds could be heard but I could hear the life outside. Everyone outside was alive and up except us three. Slowly, I dragged my tired body out of my head, took the towels and gown and headed off to the bathroom. The warm shower woke up my senses and all I could remember was how it felt good to have talked rather than listen. A heavy silver metal dustbin lid had been allowed to be taken off and somehow all the garbage had been recycled and the sin was almost empty and rid of all the bad things. End of the old year!

New Year's Day and it was as if that same party was in full swing again by the evening. There was something different today. There was no smell of food being cooked or the noise of dizzy bubbles popping, but slowly there were the local families coming and today it was not just men but then women as well. We do not have any relatives here, but our neighbours are our family. Lots of young girls in their best frocks, ladies with their respected veil on and men in their crispy, starched and well-ironed suits and then there was Kaka and me in our flip flops still and when Father did manage to come downstairs, he too had his flip-flops on. We were both told by Father to put on our "nice" clothes and he told me not to talk about the "elections" today with anyone as that was all I did do and the second thing was not to wear the "silly veil" on my head like a grown-up. I did not make a comment but just arched my eyebrows at what he had said.

His words in my ears, I headed off to her bedroom and took her sari that she loved. It was one of her best saris, red with tarnished gold round circles. It was fit for a princess. I tied it tight and made it hug my body tight. The waist was bare and I put a jingling belt around my child-like waistline. It was the first time that my waist was bare and I tossled my hair into curls and pinned it to the left side of the neck and pinned a red flower to keep it in place. I sat at her dresser and plastered on her make-up as close as I could get to looking like her and then, I stood against that big mirror. I didn't want to see her, so I slowly looked on from the side, but I couldn't see her at all, so I looked at her head-on but still the girl in front of me was not her. I took the ends of the long scarf part of the sari and put in on my head. I pulled it to cover the full head, moved it half way back and then, I saw what I wanted to see. She was there in front of me.

I walked elegantly into the room which was full now and it was like the room of the royal banquet. It had been served with waiters looking new and fresh with Kaka and Father both chatting away. Guests mingling with one another and then as their ears listen to the music it all goes silent as they all turn their heads, the one hundred and one eyes stood and stared. My father ushered the waiters to serve more drinks so that the eyes would no longer peer over their half-empty glasses and he waited for their hands to start waving the empty cocktail sticks with remainders of olives and pineapple, whilst the juice drips onto the floor but they stand motionless peering at me. Father quietly clears his throat nervously and comes straight at me. "Meera dearest, what's all this?"

"What do you mean, Father?"

"I told you to be yourself, not a double of your Mother and what's all this palava with covering the head? Be a girl, a young child not a woman acting like a mother or married woman. Oh God, Meera, please, please."

"Is this the first time that you have actually noticed what I am wearing Papa, the first time ever Papa? Tell me, is this the only reason why you are noticing me, what I am wearing on my head,

151

Mother's veil, is that the only thing that you can see? Can you not see the real Meera underneath it and anyhow, Mama always wore it and you never disliked it so now, this is me. I wear the veil and you notice me and yet Mother wore it and you didn't notice her. What is that about, do girls have to wear the veil to get noticed? Are we no one without it or half of a person of half-heartedly and half respected only?"

I carried on and on and he put his head down in shame and I know that he was quiet only because he didn't want to create a fuss or be ridiculed in front of his friends. This was a party for the selected few who were going to get Father elected again and I know, that the only reason why the Coke can ring was given to me was, because he was the elected one by the idiots outside. I was going to be used as the ladder by him to climb onto, so to reach his elected ego. How strange is that and how can a single Coke can ring have so much power? How can the power of the elections be so controlling that people would be willing to do whatever was needed, to reach the top? The look on Father's face had lifted the clouds away and yet I didn't know what direction I should be heading towards but, my head was full of wondering questions.

Quietly, without even a shudder, I brushed against his cold arm and went straight to Noddy. He was standing so very upright and tight-lipped next to his father, so I assumed. Drinks started flowing and conversations started mingling with

152

one another. I stood silently with Noddy whilst he kept talking to the group he was standing with. I listened and they all talked and it was all about the elections, the elected and the losers.

"I know about losers, my father is a loser."

"Meera, he didn't lose this election."

"I didn't mean just at the elections, he has lost in life, loser."

"Meera, you cannot speak to your father like that, no child can speak to their elders in that way. I daren't speak to Father like this."

He spoke and I just saw the empty space with lots and lots of people in it who were too busy to even notice this empty space, clear and white, unstained. I look directly at the cracks on his forehead and know, that he has lived his life, after all he is no Spring chicken so Kaka said. He must be at least mid-thirties and I focus on those cracks and yet I can smell her all around me, her bodily scent and yet, what I see, no one else does. The memories of her body lightly flowing in this thin clean cloth and her feet, soft like a feather used to glide across this tiled floor, so how would anyone hear her or see her? You need a heart to hear this not your eyes.

The room is just an empty space and yet it isn't so empty. I tell her in a soft whisper that I crave to lay in her arms yet again, soothingly against her womanly body and she always tells me how perfect I look, once I have her make-up plastered on with the spades and trowels that were made for it. The tears, unlike the empty air lay heavy and burdened and every night, I can hear her cry or is it someone inside of me? I am tired of hearing my own voice again and again, but I convince myself that there is not going to be any more of this, and tomorrow, I plaster a thick smile on my lips and hopefully the tears won't roll and by now, I don't know if I have told Noddy all this or just myself. Soon enough I can see my father going to the front of the room and he tinkers his drinks glass with a spoon to get everyone's attention and mine as well. He asks me to come to him as he holds out his hand and his arms stretch long and big, straight to my throat and yet we are standing far from him. I walk with one hand tugging gently to the veil to make sure it stays on, and the other hand, my right hand, gently swinging beside me.

Noddy follows behind me and even though I cannot see him moving behind me, I can sense him whilst this empty air carries him closer and closer to me and there is a lemon citrus kind of smell that has cradled his facial skin and I can, almost see it in between his shaven hairs. We both stand side-by-side and Father in the middle. Father likes speaking and I like to listen. He used to speak to her, soft voices amongst the small gestures of affection. I liked to listen to her. She said things that I could hear myself saying in later years and then some of us are born to talk and there are those of us who always had to listen. Slowly but surely, I have been raised in that way and with that in my head firmly, I stroke my ears. Am I turning into my mother?

The veil on my head like second skin and second nature, I have gotten used to wearing it, lady-like clothes, like the lady who wore them before me and over six months have gone by and within this period, Father has not bought her any new clothes. Maybe he feels that she doesn't need them anymore and then there is me, I have found two six-feet wardrobes full and the veils, a ray of sunshine. The sunshine holds living things together and connected. The assorted veils for the one who wears them now and the exploitation of the innocent outside people helplessly overpowered by the ones who survived on power, to them it is the only way for survival. Noddy is one of those.

The elected men and the veiled women, but not all of them are veiled, so why is it some do and others don't? They all look perfectly made-up. Clothes pressed, lips outlined, black kohl lines, slick straight around the eyes and from the inside, the perfect black and white ball cunningly looks on. My eyes a bit runny, smeared and a bit inexperienced. The anger and sweat and tears have marked the make-up somewhat but I had other things on my mind. Standing here in anticipation as I can see the corner of my veil shaking nervously all alone. Somehow I heard the words surrounding the chilled air in the background, rather than here next to me. With a big gleam in his eyes, he announced that Noddy and I were officially getting engaged today and the rings, will be placed on each other's finger in front of all and as food and drink was still flowing, the cake will be cut after the exchange of rings and the wedding would be very, very soon.

The only thing that I can remember telling Father was that I was only sixteen and had not even finished my study as yet or even learnt to live without Mother yet and that he needed me to be with him and like an ignorant man, he ignored all my pleas, he gently smiled and replied "Don't worry Meera, I have Kaka." That summed up the illusion that I was under and the meaning of my life. I had no more to say. Everyone seemed to be having fun with their real tanned skins and their fake smiles and their loud noises in a perfect world, but this was not it. The Coke can ring was tied on the corner of my veil and it was safe there in a tight knot as I took it out of the knot, my tear glistened on it. The exchanging of rings from the dampened eye and the closed tight mouth and the refusal to eat the cake from anyone's hand and still the cheering crowds delighted their stomachs. The wild night continued as the early birds' eyes peered into the cold darkness outside. It was cold and dark all around me now.

New Year's Day, news for the first day of the first month and I know that this is the way it's always going to be. It used to be for Mother as well as New Year's Day parties were always traditional and at times, she peered only through the cracks of the doorway with her hand carefully spread out on the side wall and her heart fluttering with his absence. There were times when she would go and join in but there was only talk of the man's talk and then she was the loner and now he is and me too. I peered with my dark eyes into the night's darkness on a future where winners have it all and that was life's way of life. Everything outside and in here everything was so very silently still.

Chapter 7

The fog had lifted and the air should have been light but instead, it had become heavier and I was drifting from the unknown to the known, but I did not know what direction I should be taking. I chose to listen to Father. New Year's Day and new decisions and the talk of the new life. I spoke to great lengths. Kaka listened but stayed silent and all Father could say was, that girls should be married once they come of age and that only, yes, only mothers can look after daughters and that he works and is out a lot of the time and feels worried for me as there is no one who can take care for me whilst I am alone at home, every day.

They were all poor excuses in a very wide opened mouth and as we sat and talked on the second round and the third and the fourth and on the fifth day of this new month it had made no difference to his decision. He went on to explain there was a bundle of envelopes, cream satin envelopes with wedding invitations inside which I had ignored on the side table and because I had left early I did not see everyone leaving with the wedding invitations under their arms. "Well at least the wedding will be much later on in the summer I presume, Father" was all I could add. Up to this point he had been looking straight at me but now his eyes looked very genuine in what he was trying to say and there seemed to be this quest for the questions to be answered and instead of replying, his gaze lifted from my face to concentrate on the rug on the floor and the stains blotching the flowers on this piece of wool.

He did not look up and in silence turned his head to Kaka and Kaka knows exactly what Father is trying to say without him uttering a single word. Kaka gets up, goes to the side table and gets the envelope and hands it nervously to me. Instantly, I take it and this envelope was rather special, unlike me or maybe just like me, expensive and beautiful. I did not want to know the date of my fate and I am sure I would find out sure enough. Better that, than now.

The following day, Father, Kaka and some of the outside people and a couple of the regular workers like Maria had come in the afternoon and we were busy with the marigold and rose flower garlands, stringing the delicate flowers into the delicate lives with a thick needle and one by one arranging them along the stairs that take people from one destination to their ending dream. The balcony and the big hall in the middle looked like the setting of a dream wedding; fresh assortments of flowers put into decorative vases neatly into the corners and the jasmine scented smelly sticks lit around the hall.

Maria kept singing of the joy and the tribulations of a wedding and how lucky I was to get a man like him and on and on.

Father sensed that the ice had been broken gently and cleverly and so he simply asked me to go and put something nice on as guests would be arriving for dinner. People, almost like strangers started to gather their bodies into this big empty space, handing me gifts and money and their royal handshakes and then without much of a stir, they tucked into the food and now it was almost quite real that it was New Year's Day. Noddy's family came and we both spent some time together and the adults did what they do best. I dressed up and against Father's approval I wore Mother's veil but this time from the tip of my head all the way to the back like a woman, not a girl. Another four days of all this hustling and partying continued and on the 9th January, everyone talked about the wedding tomorrow and what they will be wearing and the timetable for the day. Maybe the penny just dropped.

It was 10 o'clock on the dot, on the clock in the big hallway and the house smelled of flowers, a strong pungent smell of almost lilies and there were so many colours all over the house, but only downstairs really. My life did not feel colourful at all nor did it smell joyful, but I had excepted the fact that this was it and strange as it may seem, it was as if I was living my mother's life and as if the years had taken me back to the time of when she had got married and how it would have been just like this. I left everyone to it and like a fly on the wall that everyone sees but does not acknowledge, I opened that luscious envelope. My fingers felt lifeless and limp as I began to come to terms with the big day tomorrow.

By 9 o'clock in the morning I was ready to tick

tock like the clock as the invitation card had intended me to do so and as I looked out of the mother's window, maybe for the final time and all dressed up, I see a familiar face of a young girl entering the gate and I wonder how from that day till now I had grown and we had both part. I rushed to the hallway balcony and I hear her words, hello, my name's Marilyn, Marilyn Monroe. Maradonna told me that she lived here so I thought I would check her out, is she in. Father was feeling jovial and replied, "Good day to you young lady hope you are well. Maradonna right, Maradonna is a guy, a footballer so you must be in search of a footballer not a girl. I am sorry but there are no boys living here. Now if you have come for food or clothes or money, you have come to the right house, you're welcome to take some things home, no problem."

She kept insisting her truth and Father didn't really reply and as her words felt as if they were uttered in the distance now, creating a lull dull echo. I ran back to Mother's window and there she was. Rania or Marilyn Monroe as she wants to be was being taken to the gates. There was disappointment and pain in her face to have been let down once again and with no expectations but unlike the girl I met once before. Her face told the story of how I had lied to her and I didn't want her to be let down by yet another person this time I had a choice. She would have lost faith once again so quickly I get up from my seat and go close to the open window. I keep waving with my left hand, the one with the coke can ring on it.

For a few moments she looks and then turns away and then heads towards the outside of the gates, she was leaving with nothing and not even the truth. "Marilyn Marilyn" I shouted and I waved faster and faster and as my words reached her ears and my hand reached her heart she came back into the drive and with the tiniest squint in her eyes she looked up at me.

"I'm coming," she shouted back with a big grin. I ran downstairs in the clothes that had been laid out for me. Carefully draped wedding clothes, red and rosy and the heavy expensive antique jewellery that stood still in time just like me and then I caught myself looking in the mirror. I could see Mother with the plastered on make-up and she was looking right back at me in all her glory, the make-up, jewellery and her clothes and of course her veil. Oh god, this was her wedding dress. The front door was open and quite often this is because the gate outside is always closed and so, we always have a little bit of the outside sunshine indoors every day, unless of course it is cold and somehow there was no chill now even though it was winter because the big red bright sunshine stood there, Marilyn.

"Meera, Meera, where are you going?" Father uttered in shock.

"Papa, it's Marilyn Monroe, well wanna be Marilyn MONROE. Rania is her real name and Rani, like our own rani is what she is called. You know that girl I told you that I met that day when I

162

went out for the day and I got wet and I had fun, remember, remember, and you didn't believe me, now you do, right Papa, right Papa?"

"RIGHT, Meera, right. I am sorry dear that I didn't believe you dear but let's put that in the past and move on, today is a great day so invite your friend in and ask her to stay with you, you will need her, I mean a female you will need today. Hey she could be your bridesmaid, your best friend." Those words had some truth and yet promise and optimism in them. "By the way Meera why was she asking for Maradonna?"

"PAPA, it's Madonna, the singer, I told you that day."

"Of course you did girl, of course you did, Maradonna is Madonna." With these words he started to laugh hysterically at the thought of how innocent and naive and childish we both were, me trying to be Madonna even though I couldn't even dream of singing and then her, not even pronouncing it correctly, what a Maradonna or Madonna shambles he cracked in laughter, shambles. I know that is what he thinks and then, of course, he must be thinking that this young woman is introducing herself a Marilyn Monroe and not as rania or rani for short but is in complete and utter make belief land by calling herself by a beautiful icon, the one and only Marilyn Monroe, could there possibly be more than one, ever. He laughingly continued and I could see the joyful tears reaming down his eyes and rather than being upset with his joking and mocking or whatever, I

163

could see the funny side of it and quite frankly it was nice to see him laugh, for once. I had not seen him laugh in a very long time. It was a sheer joy to watch.

I went outside to greet her and we both hug one another like best friends do especially those who need someone, but still being wary of the fact that my dress was pressing hard against my flesh and the diamonds were pushing into my skin and felt a little uncomfortable but that didn't matter what so ever. Papa looked at me as if the weight had been lifted off his shoulders because finally I had someone; a real person who was here for me. A female I could talk to, share my grief with or share conversation with and I did like it.

A rich kid was getting married and clothes were being handed out as a tradition and lots of free food and drinks were available on tap she said but once inside, we went straight into my bedroom and even though we could hear lots of noises of the pitter patter noises on the hard floor, more than that, we could smell the wind with its ooze of warming smells of the food with its uncountable calories. Marilyn told me that she only came here today because she was told by the outside people about it. Her purpose of being fed for free and taking enough for parents as well was the plan from the 'Rani bungalow' and suddenly as she rang the bell, that name made her realise that one day some lost forlorn girl had mentioned that name and the fairytale stories of the rich kid who told so many porkies and even at that point, she had no faith in my story and I knew for a fact that her stories were webs of fiction and it was just as well that I was looking out, otherwise my so called lies would have remained just that.

We started off from where we finished off that day and then I told her about the elections, this veil and the many changing colours of Mother's veil and the coke can ring and about today. I gave her the card and after reading it herself, all she could say was "Oh wow, how brilliant, if only I could get so lucky, my parents cannot work so I have to, they are not well so I have to look after them and fear for them all day, we do not have anyone to turn to or ask. Our relatives think that if they talk to us we will only ask for money, so it's easier to avoid us than face us, this way they are not dying and I am not living so how and when, would anyone ask for my hand in marriage and no one has. I mean I ain't met anyone who I can ask to marry me and anyhow, what would I offer them?"

She stated the obvious and sometimes the most obvious things always cause the most pain, so deep down inside, but she quickly brushed off that doom and gloom and started to go through the clothes, jewellery and make up and perfumes. I told her that she could wear anything that she fancied as some of it belonged to Mother and the rest was alien to me as well. She picked up the different colours and the different styles and fashion and couldn't believe in my luck and then finally she picked something so very similar to what I was wearing. We found her some jewellery and slapped the same make up on. Two peas in a pod that was how we looked and yet on our own, I looked like Mother but with Marilyn we both looked almost like sisters.

I could hear Father calling us in his joking mood "Would Marilyn and Madonna like to accompany us, if of course we're not expecting too much." He had his laughable tone in his speech; we were having too much fun to let the wedding or anything else get in the way. There was a big marquee in the back court yard and the guests were there from one end to the other but not upstairs or the store room that held together all extra things that were spare. She wasn't spare and even though that room was open, but not bare and yet, I could hear the walls breathe.

Breath, I had to take a deep breath and I do not like to go into that room any more, not even to get cans of food or drink but then I am wearing a can ring off one of those cans in that room. No matter how much I tried to shy away or hide or even despair, I cannot cut myself away from that room or myself or Father. The wedding ceremony was fine, reception was good and then all of a sudden it was evening time and I did not even know where the day had gone. I did know that it really was time to go to the new house and today it was my turn and all the things that had become a big part of my life and yet, they were almost a daze as if they were far too trivial to bother about and all because of Marilyn. I hope I never wake up or break up with her for she has been the best thing in my life ever but as I threw the handful of rice for prosperity sake over my head and on to the guests lining behind me, she was still beside me and I could see her but felt that someone even dearer was even closer to me.

On the other side, but who exactly? I don't know and then there was Father, full of wise words and his big hug were all left plastered tightly against my body as I cradled in to the Range Rover. It had red and blue ribbons on it and with Noddy on one side and Marilyn on the other, it felt perfect and someone like me, right next to me and all I wondered was, I wish life could stay like this forever. The chauffer drove off with Noddy's father with us. I could see papa standing against the gate sobbing silently with his white handkerchief and the sly companion by his side.

Soon enough the car stopped, it was only about half an hour drive and we talked all the way whilst Noddy looked out of the window and then we came into a house that was guarded by a bigger, taller gate and a guard who stood staring at it and as the house shined a whole lot more than ours, it has lots of mirrors and clear crystals and you could tell that it was a well-kept house. It was modern and there was no Kaka but then there were maids but I think workers sound a bit better. All the rituals were done by Noddy, his father and their family and all the work by the outside ladies and yet, they were not the outside people, so it wouldn't be fair to call them outside people, so workers seem fairer. Life should be fair.

Noddy told me to take Marilyn upstairs and we could both rest and sleep together in my new bedroom. He showed us my new bedroom and it was to the back of the house, like my old room at Father's house. He was no longer Papa but my father, but I could not enter it. He asked what was wrong and I added that I can no longer sleep at the back of the house. I could only sleep facing the front like Mother's bedroom. We were shown two rooms that faced the front main street and the one that had the most light coming into it from the street lamp and lots of natural light with windows made of stained glass and the shutters, as we had in Father's house.

My eyes searched for Mother's favourite thing, that swinging chair, she sat on that the last time and all the times before that as well. I needed to look out of the window like she always did, I needed that almost as if it was a woman thing that females did. I asked if they had one and I knew that there had to be one here as anyone with a bit of money always had one, but there were no females so maybe the men didn't have one. Noddy scratched his head and there was great silent awkwardness in the still air and then he took his right finger next to his thumb and started poking his temple as if he was shooting it.

"Just wait." I looked on without moving and then he gently ushered me to go and at least sit on the small sofa and wait. We both sat on the bed and waited patiently and in silence whilst looking around and observing the intricate details of this room. You could tell this was a visitors room, unused un-abused and so now and then came a wooden knock on the side of the door and two men with orange turbans walked with a very modern swinging chair. It was golden and really quite beautiful and I knew that I could grow to love it. It wasn't her but it was and could be, mine. Noddy told them to place it at the end of the bed but I told him that it had to be in the same place as Mother's, in front of the window. Now it looked like home and whilst I sat and got used to seeing this as mine, we both laid on the massive queen size bed whilst the workers brought things in and in and in. It was beginning to look more like my room and my house.

The sun was full of crispy clear sunshine like the crackle of Doritos shining straight the glass window and the shutters were still open from last night. It just looked so beautiful and as I admired just as I used to before, this tender aged girl sleeping next to me dead to the world as if she had not slept in a long time. I kept looking at her as she looked like a peaceful child with her mouth open with a sweet smell, her legs and arms crouched together and her hair rugged like a street girl, which she was. Her hand nails showing remainders of all the food that she over ate last night and toe nails showing the remains of her lived life. I could see a tiny lump on her stomach because of the large amount she had eaten for breakfast, lunch and supper of the day before.

The street kid in rich kid's clothes and here and

now the girl who sleeps rough on her string woven bed with the hollow wooden posts and now all that mattered lay fast asleep on a princess's bed. There are no tattered grease marked sheets with empty pillows, far from it, the Egyptian cotton sheets with the thick snug duvet half cradling her petite body and her hard, dusty coarse and crusty baked feet. She could of done with more flesh but then she was a real street kid, they are trained to eat if and when and not as a habit of eating three square meals and as I continue looking at her, it's obvious and clear like the listening windows in this house that she is a kid, who doesn't need any of us but we do and she only has a need for herself. She is a defender for herself, eating when she has whatever food and eating till no more can possibly fit in her tight taut little sack, wearing and sleeping whenever, tightly and lightly after hunting down people for their money and their uses. It is sheer hard work.

She has so many lines which have not turned into wrinkles as yet and the worrying lines that her forehead has searched for, and the cracked dimples just above her so perfect eye brows show the sews of her own safety, her tatty string like coarse hair show how very little it got combed and it is always better to comb than brush and then her feet and hands from the miles that she has walked barefooted to the tons and tons of hard graft her tiny hands have done, and all under the scorching Mother Nature.

She finally wakes up with the smiling sun in her

smile and rubs her eyes like a little kid and whilst twisting from side to side, her baby like body almost as if she cannot believe where she has woken up, still almost in a daze. "How could lady luck be on her side?" she wondered. "Oh Maradonna, oh my God it's morning already, I only meant to doze for a little while not sleep the whole, oh my God, NIGHT. It was the best sleep ever but, but.... I have to go as my poor parents they must be worried sick they probably have called the police and searched and called people to hunt me down and I am sure that they never slept all night long and the beds wont have been slept in or made today and the worry for my safety and they were all alone and whilst I laid here in comfort, they probably drooped over their sunglasses in a hope of seeing a glimpse of me, worried and wonders of my whereabouts. You know it's never safe on the streets and now I have to go.

Please can you ask someone to go and show me the way home. I know your Noddy will know where I live, men in politics know whereabouts of all, come." I hardly heard her words but did remember her face and how peaceful she was but now, she frantically got up and found her feet firmly onto the floor and in a slow dash she headed towards the bedroom door, shouting "Noddy, Noddy, Noddy."

Noddy was downstairs and as we both looked over the hallway balcony. There he stood in a white traditional suit as the groom should be the next day but we were both still in our wedding clothes as if Noddy had married two girls yesterday and both wanting his attention but one, who was loud but quiet and the other a guest but calling the shots. He was loud and full of laughter and so was Marilyn. She started talking to him and explaining where she lived and he seemed to know the alley where her house was and the shop it was close to and the big road that led off to the street and into the alleyway where she lived and the house near the house that so and so lived and who is the uncle of so and so and as if they were already friends. Friends of the outside people, Lakeed, Sultana and all of those tit tat people out there but, no she couldn't fit in to that same group that I don't have any real contact with, no, she was definitely like me.

Noddy told Marilyn to freshen up and she needed that, a good scrub under the shower that she probably never has had as she said she had only ever had a bucket wash and after that, he said we need to come downstairs to eat and then he will drive her home. "What!? Drive as in your car?" her face was delightful.

"Yes Marilyn, drive you home and you know what Marilyn Monroe if it really makes you that happy then maybe our dear Madonna can join us and then, your family can also take a little tour around the town in the big car whilst seeing the big place with all its big sights. I think that might be a really good idea."

That seemed perfect, Marilyn explained. She

knew that her parents would never believe their luck as they have never been inside a big car. They have sat in a taxi and a rickshaw and on a bike and a moped and quite a few times on a bus. From near home to the doctor and back and that is a back breaking job all by itself. She kept repeating how amazed they will be as to why a big person would allow a little person to ride in their car for free as that doesn't happen in the real world out there. For them she went on that it would be more amazing than winning the rations for the year or enough wheat for the next six months or even get given a few big bags of rice for nothing. Their joy she said will show in their tears as that's all that they have plenty of. Their rippled skins would stretch even wider and the hollow cheeks would be filled with joy rather than emptiness, as they will peer out of their finger-marked glasses tainted with life.

We both got ready and we packed a few suits for her to take home into a huddled up sheet and I told her that she could have any of them except for Mother's veils. And I promised her that the next time that she visits I will get her lots more. I also asked her to help herself to the some of the makeup and especially face creams to protect her skin. She snarled back that people don't have time to protect one another let alone the face, it has no value as how you look has no bearing on real life itself. Instead, she grabbed a few sandals and jewellery bits and like a washer woman twinned the corners together like a delicate piece of pastry.

We both headed off to the malty smelling main room downstairs and then all ate breakfast as quickly as our mouths would allow us.

Noddy gave the driver clear defined instructions with the priority being that we should have a really good time and no complaints. We headed towards the big car; her head was clearly way above her weighed down shoulders. She kept stroking the seats and smelling the leathers and gloating at her luck as I kindly kept smiling and all the while, kept an eye on my coke can ring which kept its promise and respect today, whilst being seated next to the lazy watch around my wrist.

I kept looking at the minute hand and somehow it just felt as if the journey was much longer now than last night. Forty five minutes later, we started to arrive through the tiny gullies and alleys and meanders full of memories and the narrow walkways and rotten mud pathways with human and animal faeces and wholesome spit from the man who cares not about the others, especially those who are the inside people. We needn't worry as we don't tread these paths often. Just as well that there are so few cars around here as leg mobility is of importance and the lack of financial support means that there is no need to build paths bigger than a swinging cat.

We hardly spoke in the car and the look on Marilyn's face told us that I should not ask too many questions and except nothing in return. I understood that and the mannerism was to just keep quiet and stray our wondering eyes that is till she snapped, 'stop here!' The driver did as she told him to. She told him to wait in the car but he clearly ignored that and quickly got out of the car and opened the back passenger seat door and out flocked two young maidens. He shut the heavy squeaky door and stood beside it as if someone was dying to get inside it. Marilyn took my hand and pulled me along.

Mother was all her exciting squeakiness could usher and right there in front of us stood the cracked muddy pavement with the broken stones and hardened earth. It hadn't rained in days. Strange how I have only realized that now. There were tiny bits of food trodden on and tea leaved gathering more dust and the washing laying idly on the dry prickly branches whilst watching the passengers going by as they quietly whistled in the wind. There was so much clutter and a mud hut in the corner, but in front of me was a tiny house with two wooden shutter windows and a door that led to a dark and dusky environment that had seen harsh weather environments in its time. All of them opened into the unknown darkness set within and proudly held this family together.

The darkness of the light outside twinned with the natural daylight in the faraway horizon all shined on the small oil lit lantern with its tiny wick flickering away like a slow drive into the desert. Life was flickering with hardly any steam just like the couple that occupy this tiny hibernation. Old rumbled up words came flickering out from an old woman's bewithered tongue and she looked the perfect picture that I drew in my tiny mind, she didn't disappoint. She stood with her hands clasped tightly on her hips and her thick goggles that showed her the distance to her horizon and she sees us and slowly she pulls her sari around her wee waist full of thin rippled skin and bones that had no flesh to protect them. No veils here then.

Her hands showed her perfect age and hardship and beside her came and stood the feeble yet raw man of the house. He aided himself to the twisted walking stick as I stared at his thick white hair and then I looked at her extra thin withered away waist length plaited hair and I realize that they have noticed me staring at them so I take my eyes off them but still could feel the twigs and broken strands in the cloth of her sari. Marilyn was standing still, a bit emotional to say the least until the woman's eyes dampened and she smiled through the gaps of her teeth. The hollow and dimpled mouth was wide as the tear streamed openly into the crackled open mouth. She kept repeating, thank goodness your back rania, thank goodness and the old man thankfully just kept nodding peacefully. Marilyn wrapped them both in her arms and told them that I was her friend and she stayed the night with me, they nodded agreeingly.

The mum was very inquisitive and all she registered in her head were Marilyn's words but repeated the same dialogue of where do you live and you must have a nice house over and over again and then because I didn't really reply to her

176

statement and not really knowing why she did say what she did, but she blurted in a genuine tone, 'its ok, rania tells us these stories all the time.' Marilyn went into the black room and pulled behind her a rope woven bed almost as big as a king size bed and let it drop onto the muddy ground and then, with all her might she started slapping the dust off its threads.

She ushered me to sit on it and so did she, followed by her parents. Her mother's one leg dangling limply off the bed and the other actively under the breast of her body whilst her father huddled both of his legs into his palms and sat motionless staring into my eyes and then, onto the sodden ground where his wife had not flattened the cracks out properly. That was a woman's job and he was a real man. I smiled and he didn't but I kept looking at his grey to the morning dust clothes and the renewed hope in his thoughtful eyes. 'Do you have bulbs in your house?' and all I could think was that where in the world were his thoughts. 'bulbs, what do you mean?' he knew exactly what he meant and he continued with his short statements asking about the electricity and gas and how one day they too will have all these very, very soon. Hope had been installed in their minds properly and I think that this was good as they had something to look forward to and yet I don't even think that they had an idea about when they would have these luxuries but life for them was the only hope.

He started to tell me, with a big smile, that

Marilyn once purchased a real light bulb and soon when they do have electricity then will need it then and that they have a small gas bottle ready and waiting, also brought by her for when they get a gas stove. He knew that I wasn't impressed so he simply uttered that what would the point of having electricity when in fact the government only give a few hours of it to the poor public and the rich get access to it all of the time. He said life was all about having or not having money that was it.

"Well at least we are lucky because we don't have to pay any bills at all other wise where would we get that kind of money from to pay such big bills." I started to look at Marilyn as she was getting a bit cross eyed at his comments but didn't want to sound rude in front of them and so I asked her if she wanted to go out for a ride with the parents.

"Who is Miriam?" Mother asked Marilyn and Marilyn rudely asked her to shush. Mother asked the same question again and I watched on as Marilyn's flustered face became agitated to the point of where she rudely snapped and howled at her telling her that it is Marilyn not Miriam and with that the mother looked even more confused than before and so said, well who is she as that's all she was asking! Marilyn ignored her and told them both to go and get ready as we were all going out for a drive in the big car.

Their eyes moved from left to right and back and forth and the smile wide from one ear to the other as she calmly told her bewithered husband that he was ready as men are always ready and that she was going to go and get ready. She went quickly into the darkness and I could hear her singing in the darkness and a spray of some sort hissed away and then the creaky door opened a little further and as Marilyn looked at her mother's lips pouting with thick red lipstick and matching ping blusher stuck in between her dimple and the natural ripples and not even on the cheek boned but nearer the bottom of the face. She told her that she should always keep the door wide open and let the natural light in so she can actually see what she's doing. The mother took no notice and I am sure she didn't even hear any of it as she held lightly the small bottle of ponds cream and with a continuous downward motion she caressed her neck abruptly with no care for real life at all and then simply added that darkness was a part of their everyday life. She continued plastering her hands with the same cream.

We all move over to the car and the man waiting to escort us in to the lime light and I felt as if we were the sly foxes who had licked all the cats cream in a quick dash with our proud smiles and as the outside people passed us by we looked proud and as they looked on at the car and us, we cast our eyes to the car so that there was no way that they should miss the car and us who were going to ride in it now. People moved idly from here to there with no real means but they did all have a place to get to, where ever that was. The heat continued beating heavily on the firmed skins of all even though it's still a wee bit chilly in the mornings but everyone is relieved with the cool airs that we get blessed with first thing in the morning and no one here ever stops because of the weather. We were not scorched from the weather because we were standing proud and nothing could spoil this joyous moment. Smug smiles spread with cunning glances cutting the edges of the jealous eyes as the outside people would be like that so I thought and right now I felt that I was one of them.

After waiting and waiting and some sly shuffling in between, the lady of this house came back out with a metal silver glass and offered me a drink. I slowly looked into the solid grey mould and because I wasn't a fan of squash, I hesitated and quickly she looked at me and nodded her head as to say hurry up and drink. I paused but didn't want to seem rude so I put my nose into the glass as to look as if I was actually drinking it, which I wasn't and yet I could smell that it wasn't even the Robinson orange squash or Ribena or strawberry cordial but this was a strong almost pungent smell of rose. It was as if I was drinking rose petal juice. I held my thought there till she was convinced that I was drinking it, even though I wasn't, and then she turned her back to me and quickly I moved the metal vessel away from my mouth and sling the liquid over the back. The driver looked a bit quizzed and as I looked at where the red liquid had landed realized why he looked so confused. The red liquid was all over the car. This red liquid cannot do anyone any harm! Quickly I thanked her for it and she waved her hand to say that I was welcome to the drink.

Finally we four people were now huddled near the car and Marilyn standing so close in between her mother and me and the more that I tried to let her mother into the car the more she tried to push me afar and guarding her mother. I didn't understand why she was being so protective and as I slowly moved aside to let Marilyn get her mother into the car. I looked at the burning sod and saw what she tried so hard for me to ignore. She noticed me looking on and quickly she sharply elbowed me out of the vision of the white, turned grey flip flops with the middle scissors part broken and a struggling foot trying in vain to climb in without losing its dignity and pride. Just like her. Slowly with her face going a bit red she put her other foot on top of it to hide it so that I would not notice it so I put on this big smile as if I noticed sweet nothings by playing a nice ignorant game and without a flicker, she instantly gets in. She swallows a big lump in her tiny throat.

The middle part of her flip flop drooped out of its hole, lifeless, helpless and out of its own control, the same as the woman who laid in the middle of the swinging chair, just as helpless and emotionally out of control from the woman inside now to the woman who laid bare to the swinging throne, both of them helpless and dependent on someone else and on society, what can she do and what could she have done? Absolutely nothing as they live in the hands of others and both broken in

181

life. I hope my veil is on.

She stepped in like royalty and then just behind her I could see the old black griddle in the old smoky smoggy, London sky of the yester years but then this is not London but India and here, they light the fire daily to cook on any way and I can smell the smoke and the firewood and the puffs of the wind blown out from within the women and their empty barren chests and then she sits and strokes the clean seat with her own sari. The pots all clean with the base covered in clay to protect it from burning just like the sun protector. The line of six metal plates and the steel glasses line up ready to be used, this is their wealth. There is a bar of creamy soap that's used for cleansing of people and cloth and laying on top of all that, is the cleaning cloth that lays gathering dust against the utensils and cutlery. A bucket of water lay beside it waiting to wash away the sins of life.

Mother is busily blowing the fumes from within herself onto the windows and with her elbow she scrapes the mist away to leave a big crease on the clean glass. Her nails showed the remains of what her stomach was lined with and then she shouts at her husband, "Kapil, Kapil, let the girls get you in." We try our best but it just wasn't good enough as he just didn't have the energy to push his own body high enough to reach up into the high seats of the car, he shrugs his shoulders and I can tell that he wants us to leave him alone, we do. Marilyn tries all by herself and through his shadow I can see his plastic sandals cradling his worn out feet and then some have torn flip flops on instead.

"Mother, Mother" sheepishly Marilyn uttered concerned words out and once again she ushered me out of the way and out popped her mother from the car and then with all their might they try to cuddle him into the big vehicle. They abruptly stopped and as quickly as they possibly could, they both walked him towards the roped bed and there he laid his very tired and worn out self.

"Please Madonna, please just go, just go, I'll see you another time and we will go next time please." Her words kept forcing themselves out from within the bewitched tone and I knew something was wrong but what, I just didn't know. I owed it to her so I did as she asked and so I got in to the car and just as the car door snapped itself with the lock, I noticed the dignity they both tried to preserve and I pretended not to have noticed the wet patch left by him. I couldn't even imagine how he felt or they felt as dignity and respect is their biggest pride of all. As I drove away I could see the three, sitting and waiting for me to go so they could get on with their life and restore their pride. The three beds lined together and the three people line up together and the rest is of no real relevance. The rope, the tough sandals and the worn out flip flops will lay themselves down ready to gather dust as always.

Where else would they go and what else would they do? And yet people from the inside would not be able to relate to this life of the outside people and as a married woman I too had to preserve the ace card of honour. There is no higher accolade or card than that word, so faithful now as ever before, respect, my father used it at all times, mothers believed in it totally and I have earned it through being born a female, a daughter of a well-to-do politician, and the icing on the cake, a much respected wife of a business man and self-respected family of politicians. I have to honour this and live up to it.

Marilyn's family dwelling could well have fitted into one room of ours and yet this space does not earn the honour as that is earned through other mediums and time itself. Time itself has taught me to wear and follow the code almost of respect by wearing the veil as how else will I be respected and I know that no one has told me or wants me to do this but there are no other leading ladies and so I have to take the lead as my mother did and Mother's veil is the sign of respect for me and my new and old family. With this new life I have to remember how important it really is after all what else did Marilyn's parents have and so I have to put the nonsense out of my tiny head and breath through some responsible thoughts of wisdom and forget about friendship and grow up and face real life, like Marilyn's and Madonna's.

A respected wife of a respected man and a daughter in law of a noble and humble father-in-law. Elected public people are of a certain panache and I have to fit in that mould. I have to live like her and even though I spent very little time with Marilyn but it made me feel that my soul within, my body and my brain all have to change forever and adapt in society and the only way of keeping her so alive is by wearing her veils so she stay as close as possibly can be. I used to think that the elections and all the people connected to it whether you're a voter or a participant, you are respected for what role you play in society. Some have the winning role and others don't.

The outside people will always be the outside people and the insiders remain just that and they decide our fates so in fact control our power even though we want to believe that we in fact are empowered. They are freer than us as we have to live up to certain expectations and so we are the leads on that big dog's neck. We the inside people who wear the veils and the ones whose name is crossed or ticked by them outside. They're happy as they don't have to do things if they don't want to but that may be a myth all by itself. There are some of them in this house who come get paid for their work and they leave happily and they warm their pockets with the dosh and so long as they can feed their family, they are happy. Some of them will demand their rights and won't leave till they have eaten and burped and got a bundle neatly tucked away under their arms.

Why are we so connected together and yet so far apart as it's the same as the elected and the elector or whatever, it's all the same at times, we are all peas in a pod and we are so very different yet so very much the same. But then I still have to wear Mothers' veil and yet they all don't, so does that mean that we are more respected, no it doesn't. This cloth spells out captivity, domination and acceptance of being a female, all the things I don't hate but dislike. Without being smothered, it's like living as a free bird but with the wings being cut off. The roaring success of the lives of the politicians and the excitement of politics itself and being in the know-how and the television and the news and then there's me who can only listen and watch and at the most follow along.

Destinations we all have to search for as Mother did and I will one day and everyone else as well and is destiny really to blame for our own misgivings of ending up where we least dreading being? Thick lands of wood and the fire and the roar and the on-lookers and the rituals and so on and so forth and I am feeling as if I am there right now and what is it that's made me grow up in a matter of moments, some madness have crept into my tiny brain. My tiny brain allows me to witness the urn and her place within that and my own eyes watching and not retaliating but an acceptance of how it is and yet people say she is peaceful and I wonder if they mean her or me? But then is there in fact her and me or just us and now, just me?

Without being smothered, it's like living as a free bird but with the wings cut off. The roaring success of the lives of the politicians and the excitement of politics itself and being in the know-how and the television and the news and then there's me who can only listen and watch and at the most follow along. Destinations we all have to search for as Mother did and I will one day and everyone else as well and is destiny really to blame for our own misgivings of ending up where we least dreading being?

Thick lands of wood and the fire and the roar and the on-lookers and the rituals and so on and so forth and I am feeling as if I am there right now and what is it that's made me grow up in a matter of moments, some madness have crept into my tiny brain. My tiny brain allows me to witness the urn and her place within that and my own eyes watching and not retaliating but an acceptance of how it is and yet people say she is peaceful and I wonder if they mean her or me? But then is there in fact her and me or just us and now just me?

Chapter 8

The things that tied us both together were the veils that never did belong to me as I never wore my own ever before, but now I was the new owner of them all. Her wedding dress once on her body, like the tight glove on the worn out hand and now it had fitted me like the slithering skin on the sly snake. The old life that she once left to make a new one when she married is the one that resembles mine now and no matter what she wore it was elegantly and beautifully. There was not a day that I did not see that empty hollow still look in her eyes. It was as if that mother, the wife and more so the woman had left the carcass of this empty female body. She has closed the chapter of her book and it has not even been written in yet, the empty lines in her diary stared open and wide-eyed at the hard plastered colourful ceiling and what is going to happen to the tiny pen. Weak in its looks of black and white and it sits perfectly in the middle crack of the two open pages ready to be jollied up and made use of. Everything has a purpose in life, the pen with the diary and the veil with the woman.

Her chapter closed and mine just began two days ago. It was the perfect time to open up a diary and think back whilst painting a lovely picture of the time, which inspired me to get to where I am now. The faint lines on the open pages, the pages being the world or life and the small lines going across and each and every one is the same. Life would not be worth living if it really was the same every day and so predictable, white paper, the clean unspoiled or stained life and then, the story of everyone's life gets trampled on with the ink. Some lines get emotionally spoiled and others are just too bitter to write or tell and so, the page gets turned over with just one look. Is that what life is, just a quick look over? A quick look over, trickled with stains of blood, trickling down, tiny speckles of dead life and how alive it all feels as it is unforgettable.

That first night was like the continuation of my old life. I shared the bed with her when it should have been with him but I never thought about it that day as normally I slept alone. So the first night was quite nice and then this new house was new to me and somewhere that Marilyn had never been before. I didn't even think of Father whatsoever that night and the following day, we visited Madonna's family and then real-life began. Seeing them should not have affected me but it left an empty disturbed wanting-to-help feeling, so deep inside that even after searching, I still could not tell how deep it was embedded within me. Their life simple and happy, Marilyn and her parents, a simple but respected family and then I went and spoilt it.

She lived a life full of danger and excitement and they were living a humble and harmonious life and I went and they lost their dignity and respect and Madonna felt belittled and small. In our house, my father's house, no one felt this. Were we the dignified one, the ones with the respect, or were we the ones who demanded respect from them? And then maybe "respect" may be the only humble aspect of their life that no one could ever take away from them. I had to go and ruin that as well and somehow, maybe I ruined Mother's life as well as I should have gotten to her before and as for Father, I ruined his because, I should have been born a boy because in our society, whether you are poor or rich, everyone would prefer a boy. The boy would have sat with Father talking with his mates and mingled, but I had to sit with Mother instead. I could have smoked like all of them but I never have and secretly they all drink that intoxicating stuff that I never have and so, it is the boy that gets all these privileges. Father would have had his son sitting with him, beside him and he would have showed him off instead of me hidden away, not seen or heard.

Mother died without leaving an heir to her throne so no one to take on Father's name because, a son inherits that and so, the Father's name lives forever. I'll take my husband's name but then why do I have to take a man's name? It is the accepted thing that women do. Mother took Father's name and I have to do so as well. That is the only way it is, no questions asked.

Some are leaders and people like us will always be the followers, those who watch the outside people spitting on the footpath and swearing under their breath at the fast drivers who horn loudly at those who are always on their feet. The dripping of that red smelly colour dries quickly as it runs away from the warm body and it seals itself dry on the lips of the madams and me as I used to run into the school and as the car doors shut tightly and the school gates were bolted, so have we girls bolted ourselves within the walls of our houses and then we stand arm-in-arm behind the dirty walls of this school and society. "Dirty" is not a dirty word at all as the on-looking crowd always jeer at the squeaking tricycle and the snotty-nosed kid, he's much too big to get on the bike but he controls this squeaky metal and as we look out of our windows, we point and shout at him and he thinks that this is the signal for him to come into our homes and our hearts but how wrong he really is as we wanted him "just" to keep away from us. There is so much division between us all.

"Us" is the word that she craved for, him and her and the small matter of "time" that would make the "us" complete and that just wasn't meant to be, as time heals all the scars that were embedded through her. "Us" as in me and my new husband. "Us" as in Mother and Father. "Us" as in the veil and head, the head and the respect and the slow red warm drips of life trickling down through the cold air like the icicle waiting for the temperature to rise so it can be released. I had been released from the cage into the open air of someone else's four walls, colourful, well-maintained and full of male life. There was no sign of any female life at all except for the thin one standing and the picture of a white half-naked one hanging on the wall.

A week had gone by and it felt as if the seconds had got lost and the minute hand had stood still but the hour hand on the big hall clock that overpowered the antique rustic hallway still had life in it but, I didn't know that life's wisdom has taught me all about time. The dripping of warm red life, the hair luscious and alive and then there is the clock, heavily laden by people who are forever working against time like rat or gerbils running around in their cages. I think this family is all about time, unlike our family or rather exactly like ours. If they were all about time maybe he would have known that I was married to him and I should fit into the equation of time somewhere.

There is always a lot of laughter and cheer in this house and the mood is normally loud and boisterous, as I have got to hear. Six boys and a father and a few workers, all male as well and it doesn't seem strange or uncomfortable as they mess around and it is quite nice to see that, but then I sit in-between them like Snow White staring at their big eyes and their big hand gestures and to top it off, their loud jolly conversations. I think they are all politicians as they do talk the same dialogue as their father but, there is a lot of conversation that I can't even understand.

I cannot even remember all the details of my wedding but I do know that this is my family now and anyway, I think it may not be a bad thing as it

192

would have been too quiet in my father's house. Just Father and me, but now it will be Father on his own. "His own" is a very lonely word. She was on her own when she should not have been. Some things are never meant to be alone, like the veil without a head and the girl who parades herself around the big house with her head sealed forever in the veiled garments. I think that is how it is meant to be.

I did not want to be lonely but then I was not really all alone because I did have Mother's veil. Anything I wore was totally incomplete unless it had one of her veils covering my head and only then it felt complete. I was the empty box yet to have things put into and so without the lid on the box, it just felt kind of empty and unprotected and so the veil, was the lid on top of the box that had not a lot in it. All these things are hard and calculated and without life, but I was full of life, just like this house. Every bit of her veiled cloth was very much full of life and often I feel that she was as still as the veil that laid on her head and even though it has been a while, it is still as fresh in my mind as then. I can still sense her being within my belly button somewhere, but it was hard to put my finger on any one particular part. It was easy to smell her inner bodily smell as I had not washed any of her veils at all and I could smell her beauty within the fabrics and the smell in the middle was different to the sides.

Sweet almond, smell of her neck as the cloth always draped around her tall slim neck, dusky skins with dusty cloths and dusky sky with danger of the dark mauve sky. And even when the rains come, they make the land smell and I know that my nostrils always are woken to the smells, smell of blood, the red perfumed liquid, the rats roaming freely on the streets and spreading their vermin smell around the air and the humans look on in anticipation whilst releasing juices as well. But there is a wonderful smell in this house, the smell of lavender and pine antiseptic as this is always used for cleaning. It's a wonderful clean, mountain-fresh smell and there is the smell of my new husband. He always smells of fabric conditioner and even though I know that it is not just his clothes that smell nice, his skin does as well, but I am sure that he doesn't rinse with fabric conditioner.

I flick the pages of my empty diary and of my almost empty life because what can I actually write is that, nothing is happening and yet living a married life, and aren't married people supposed to be "wedded" and what does that mean? Two people living together, two people living with extended family but I am already doing this, so what else is marriage?

"Father, can I call you 'Father'?" I say to Noddy's dad.

"Of course, I wouldn't expect anything else, dear."

"Well, Father, a week has gone by of my marriage and I have my bedroom and my clothes and things and of course my mother's veils and her

194

smell and everything and then, I kind of wonder what is marriage? I mean, I was living with Mother and Father and then with Father only and of course Kaka, you know who Kaka is, right? Yes, you do know him. Remember that day when I saw you for the first time in our house and Kaka was standing next to me and he handed tea to you in that bright red cup, him? Anyway, as I was saying, he and I and Father and Mother before that and life ticked away happily until that time and since that time.... well, since that time...."

"Carry on dear, it's nice to hear a female talk in this house, you don't know how comforting it is to hear a woman's voice in my house again after such a long time. My mother talked a lot and so did my wife but sadly both passed away at a young age and did they talk! They talked with one another from the time when the sun smiled to the time when it was too tired to smile anymore and since their deaths a few years ago, the boys have become a lot closer together and even though they cannot talk as much as the women did, they do try their best for my sake."

"Your sake, what do you mean?"

"Well dear, no matter what happens in life, at home or outdoors, the biggest joy in my life is when I am at home, relaxing and listening to the sound of words, the action of the hands and the loud smother of laughter. There is nothing as homely as that, nothing that gives me so much peace within, where it really matters, somewhere sacred within, but where exactly, I don't know? I miss the ladies in my life but I am so happy that you accepted our offer to join us to make this family go forward but not complete yet."

"Complete?"

"Yes, complete. No, I didn't mean with children or anything because I know you are still too young and you have a lot of life yet to live before all that, things to do, places to go, the world to explore. What I meant was when all the boys finally get married and have their wives here as well, then our family will be complete, only then because you know in our tradition, we all live together no matter how many or what the circumstances and that was my great-grandfather's rule and it has been the same ever since."

"So where are your brothers, or don't you have any?"

"Well, I do but they were given houses by my father and I was given one as well, this one and Father split all his wealth between all of us six brothers and told us to keep our family altogether. My brothers are all married and have their wives and children and their own business which was started with Father's help and this furniture business was given to me, see dear, all the furniture in here is all our own goods and...."

"But Father, you are a politician, aren't you?"

"Of course I am and my sons will all be in office as well soon but, the business we all run together and we have workers and politics is a man's social get-together as well."

"Man's?"

"Yes dear, it is a man's world and politics is a man's world. After all, how many women are in politics? Hardly any and it would take a long time before women get their feet under the table, but don't you worry your pretty little self about these things. The ladies in our family always stayed at home and the only time they went out was to enjoy themselves, either visiting, socializing or spending money and you too can do all that girl, but first of all, your husband Veer needs to find time in his diary and fit you in."

"Fit me in?"

"Why, well he does have to try and fit you into his life by making sure that he spends time with you being a husband, going away for a while with you and spending evenings romancing with you. I will see to it girl that he does."

"Well, Father, aren't we both supposed to...."

"Ahaaa, no, you cannot have this conversation with me girl. This is only with a woman or your husband, please understand. I don't mean to be rude. You get my point, right? You do understand, don't you?"

"Of course, but Veer's not home a lot and I don't know what to do."

"Well, how about if we ask Sunny, our Minder, if he can bring his wife in our house and do some of the chores as this way you can spend time with a woman and talk to her and ask all you like, as men's conversations are slightly different to women's and how I've missed a woman's conversation."

"Father, I just don't know what my role here is. There are only men here and it seems as if I am quite alone, there's not much to do."

"Dearest Meera, you lost your beautiful mother not that long ago. Of course, you will feel this. You are going to miss her so very much and I promise to help you whenever I can with whatever, after all you will see more of me at home than the boys. I have done the majority of my tasks in life but they are still trying to step up the ladder."

Stepladder that she sometimes used to step on and reach for the stars and now and again to get the bed linen from the drawers high above. Old memories trapped within those wooden drawers. Memories of the child following the mother in laughter and Father being protective and folded into an old century box and the old bell-bottomed trousers with the skimpy-short tight tops showing no cleavage as this little girl didn't have that much and the stilettos that would bend over backwards to get a smooth foot inside of them. But they were all the good times and a memory that was so far away. Some have all the luck and can reminisce throughout their life and others have such a short span of it that those things and these things are all just memories. And then here we are once again at that same corner of life! The red stains that will never wash away. The head sealed so no one can get to it, like hers and mine and many others and tainted with the things that go round and round. Then there is life, and I wonder what I am doing here.

He looks into the air and my eyes follow the emptiness, his words silent but I can still hear my own inside as I sit and scratch my nail. The sweet pain is nice and for a very long time now, it has been the only thing that really was real. His smile is plastered as always on his face and my face echoes the life that I should have had to live, the empty look in my eyes as reality bears a big part, the lips just don't widen enough anymore and the girl inside in search for the woman who lives silently within her. There is life outside as I can hear a car in the distance and the horn calling out to the alive persons and I think I did hear it but then am I really sure?

Veer, Georgie, Jack, Fatty and Bunny all arrive in a line, the eldest first and the youngest at the end of the line and this happens every time as long as you can remember the names, you know who is who. All tall, well-built boys or rather men as they are all older than me and in their own way, quite handsome and yet they all look totally different to one another. A week of watching the men, Father watching and observing and all the children with their happy "smiling" eyes, loud conversations and always willing to offer great expressive body language. Every time they look at me to get me involved with their talk of either sports and normally cricket and football or debating politics and of course business, the price of tit tat or bargains.

The more they tried, the more I smiled and even laughed with their laughter and this alone made me feel safe. It showed them that I was happy. As the evening showed the sky with the dusky vibes and the children all trotted inside to sleep and the maids wiped their brows and rubbed their shriveled fingers against their not-so crispy clean aprons, as the day had been done now. In here, Father's sand-like feet rubbed together to get rid of the day and all the while, I stare at the smiles around his eyes and all I can think is, what would his mother and wife have looked like and do all mothers wear a veil? I think so, that is why it is called a mother's veil.

I wear it but why the hell have I started to wear the snoope? They tie me to the past and the past is what I had, not what I want, so why do I have to care about it? The only thing that I do have is my own father and only the remains of my mother and these colourful fabrics tied her to father and now they tie me to her but part me from my husband. Father rubs his moustache and I know that even without watching him from the corner of my eye, I can see his arm moving to and fro. He is now standing and his feet slowly move from underneath the chair towards the door and then I leap up. He waves his hand as a gesture of wishing all goodnight. In a loud chorus, they bid him a goodnight and as I follow Veer with my fairy-like steps and still with my ear to the others and now the deck of playing cards have come out of the expensive chest and the crispy wafer cards ruffle within the boys' hands. The crackling of the cards and the loud snorts of the men whose stomachs are full to the rim and the happiness goes round and round as I see myself sitting on the merry-go-round and I am the only one who is actually quiet.

"Hey Veer, don't you want to talk to me?"

"Not really. I don't have to or need to talk about anything. Why?"

"Well, before the wedding, our anniversary, we talked and now a week has gone by but we are not like husband and wife."

"Don't say all this outside my room. Come in quickly and sit down."

His room, immaculately beautiful, blues and greens dancing like the wind alone, the wall and all the furniture just like the rest of this expensive house, antique and dated. His bedspread and runner spread out like the royal golden threads and there is delicacy and power in this room. Some of us carve for it and others simply don't need it. I sit on the golden cloth and stroke the beauty of it and then stroke my head. Today I am also wearing a "golden" veil. Maybe today is the perfect day for us both to be talking and.... and.... what else? What else is there that husband and wife have or do that means that they "actually" married?

"Actually, can I ask you something?"

"Well, of course," he smiled.

"It may sound rather stupid really but now that we are married and my Father and Mother were married but obviously I didn't see them getting married because I wasn't born yet.... born yet.... born yet?"

"Are you thinking what I am thinking?"

I breathe silently as I don't want him to feel the passion juices running through the pumping blood and once again I stare into the silent and still grey air. There are no tainted particles running down like shooting starts. It's clear, calm and clean and yet I am in the company of strangers who I have become a part of and yet I feel as if I don't know them. The old stranger, the newest member, the only female and the odd one out.

"Well, are you thinking what I am thinking, about being born, having children? You know.... you know what I mean, right? The only thing that I actually know was that things change when you get married but how and why, I didn't know. My father didn't talk about things like that to me and my mother always talked about what children should know rather than adult things. She didn't know what I was going to become an adult so very quickly, so quickly after her and at school we don't learn about things like that and what "that" is. I am confused about it myself, but all I know is that there has to be more than this to a married life. This loneliness has to find its way from within to the place where it can live and without the traces of what life really is.

He stands close to me now and I feel his hand stretching out to me and his feet, now so close to mine. I can feel my bottom getting heavier on the mattress and my hands stretch out wider than they possibly can and I can hear my heart beneath actually beat a hundred beats a minute. He looks into my eyes and I look at him, but not into his eyes. I feel a bit embarrassed because I don't know what I should do now. Quietly without even coughing or moving I look out of the window towards absolutely nothing.

I keep looking and at times, I can still see out of the window, at other seconds I can feel the gold threaded moments and the sheets rumble as the runner scrunches together with the rumbling and tumbling of the two foreigners as one and I didn't even know what it was all about. It was almost like the gas cooker being ignited and the flame lit and things all delicious cooked and fulfilling appetites. Why am I comparing something I know nothing about with something I am familiar with, cooking? It lasted for a good few moments, maybe minutes but it was almost like the thunder and lightning with heavy hailstones and then we lay to bear the brunt of the after-effects. Our chests heavy, hands held and clothes in tatters without trying to recollect and assemble into an orderly manner, but then it didn't seem to be an orderly thing to have done. It was ground-breaking and a bit of a fast turmoil. Undignified and unrespected.

I gather my dignity together and head for the exit of this room full of drama. He lays down and relaxes but he keeps an eye on my every flicker as dreamily he keeps his deep wooden eyes on my dark deep jet-set eyes. I put my hand onto the big golden brass knob, too big and slippery to be clutched in my palm but then in an instant my palm is twinned within his massive hairy arms, long thick black hair and then I look at my own.

There is no hair but I catch a glimpse of my arm and it does show small patches of black fine hair. I was never allowed to remove hair from any part as Mother always said that will happen when I am old enough. I wasn't old, but today I was old enough.

Enough for today, different now, everything had changed just like the time when she dripped that red liquid from within her and so the red that was on my head and now it was still on the floor. I had to save her and her dignity. Things will never be the same again. Maybe the loneliness will go and hide elsewhere, but I hope it leaves me for good as I fear it and have done so since she.... she.... she.....

I reach for the thing that will clean the shame away but he grabs me close to him and whispers sweet nothings that I don't understand. He quickly pulls the veil out of my clutches and lets it wander onto the satin red and black carpet. He is setting me free, that is how I am feeling, free and alive, and I know that I am still with strangers but all of a sudden, it doesn't feel like that anymore. The world has come together in peace, two nations reaching a meaningful end or maybe a beginning. I could not have ever imagined this as I knew nothing but for a while and even now, it feels as if I have been set free from the burden, the complications of being my lonely self.

The rest was the past as from that time he made me make his room as ours and all his worldly goods became mine. I belonged to him and all that he owned belonged to us, which included his family. All my things had been moved into this grand room and a lady had come the next day to work at our house as Father said. I had female companionship all day long till the men came home and then she left. I know she was one of the outside people but from now on, there is no division, none whatsoever between them and us or between him and me. She belonged in our house and she gave me so much joy as if I had found that mother that I lost.

The following day my father came to take me back home as it is a family ritual to take brides back to their parent's house in the evening and the following day, the in-laws come and took their thing back and then normal daily life begins. All the newly-wedded stuff falls into a routine and life starts to be lived once again. The day spent with my father was as if I had never left the home, as before, exactly the same. It was quite nice though to see how the two families of men only get on so well. Maybe I might be able to get on in the same way with both of the families. There was a traditional table of food laid out by Kaka and his Kaki and a couple of helpers, none that I could remember and we all ate together and then we moved into the sitting room and coffees and teas were served. Everyone enjoyed the treats and then his father asked if he could take me back home with him. My father humbly replied "Yes" and that was that really.

Late evening we got back home and Father retired to his grandad chair, as only he sat in that and everyone else disappeared into thin air. I went up when Veer went and as he opened his bedroom door, I wasn't sure whether the madness was over and so I should return to my own room or indeed have I got to make his bedroom my own forever? He quietly walked into his room as I silently waited and looked at the ajar door, so perfectly varnished, so glossy and unspoiled, it was almost as if I had bought a train ticket but I did not know what stand I should be waiting at and I didn't want to hither and thither as I did not want to lose my place in line and anyhow, who else is on this journey, who else has even bought a ticket and where is the train or bus or coach or even taxi, but then taxis don't really have tickets! Above all what is the destination of this ticket that I have been given and is it one way or indeed a return journey?

As I stand alone, I turn my eyes to the destination in front of me, the massive corridor with red carpeted floors and red prints streaming like the red devilish dragons putting fire on the walls. The red destination could lead me anywhere, especially places where I have been before, places where I dare not think about the colour red as it flows through my veins. Once again he makes me feel wholesome and alive as if that train ticket to nowhere really did have a destination and that ticket within me was actually worth something. Something worthwhile was how I had felt whilst Mother was alive, despite her emptiness there was joy. Despite the fact that she looked and observed and enjoyed the tantalizing joyous life even though I saw her empty eyes, there was that empty stillness in search of a need, a wanting. But no matter what, we were all alive.

I was wholesome and alive and once again I am feeling the same. He pulls me in as I can feel the prickly hair on his head as it eased against my skin and his smell that lingered on my skin since that first time that our eyes met. Eyes that met but they only look and then stray away and in here, where you see with your heart, I had seen him and sensed his bodily smell and as I take a deep breath I can smell him all of the time, the enchanted smell as I breathe deeply against his back, an almost nutty warm and inviting smell. I could even smell it whilst I slept.

We become as one yet again and again and again until two weeks had gone by and then the period of the honeymoon, five days full of marital bliss at a destination where there were hills and mountains, water and land, green lush and the bright blue sky and moments of madness with tranquility and joy. And then it, like all good things, came to an end. The wooing, the flowers after work, the chocolates before bedtime rather than milk with Ovaltine as Mother used to give us, the moments of tender madness and hurricane before the calm had all come to an abrupt end. He and I now became a routine. Every day had started now to look like another day, the calmness was reality, dinners were still hot but not sizzling anymore and the deserts were still sweet but not sweet enough. There are those of us who like the bitter side of life.

He no longer came home early to make the most of the day with me anymore. His shirts were no longer smelling of me or crispy and still as the morning and his trousers as though they were made just perfectly for him, bulging in all the right places. His mood is alive as ever before but I was no longer the center of his life. There was no emptiness in my eyes, just a longing for him. There were no tears, just the yearning of seeing him driving in through the big gates, the gates which shut the outside world against us and the gates which never really allowed them, the outside people, to enter the real lives that we lived. Them free on the outside and us trapped inside.

Early morning rush, the breaking of the sun's rays light our window as the heat bellows at us demanding us to wake up and then it is the cold showers against the naked skins and the warm soft towels against the dampened bones and the crispy clean clothes serenade us. Breakfast smells of fried bread, golden runny eggs and the sweet and earthy smells of honey, mushrooms and tomatoes and a hot spicy platter of spicy flatbreads and cooling white yogurts. The sweet smell of brewed tea and then a stern spreading of the hands over the hair and like the birds flying from the nest, they all leave.

Daytime passes with the short and sharp shopping trips and the eager waiting for Veer to come back home or at least some member of the family and the only one who did come early was Father and it was nice having him home rather than just me. We always sat and talked and many a times, Father would come home accompanied by my father and we would sit and make loose talk but they together would talk politics and I would slowly emerge into the conversation. We would talk about life and once again through their laughter, politics would give life to their mouths once again.

My father would never eat dinner, lunch or breakfast at his daughter's house but would often pop in for coffee or stewed tea. The more that my father came, the more I felt that I was able to make peace, become whole and forget or at least leave behind the past. The closer he came to me, the more I could smell Mother. The more he laughed, the more I rekindled that emptiness. The more his eyes smiled into mine, the more I could see myself in hers and the more that the sun's rays draped his mature skin, the more I could see that red colour.

It was as if he played with my emotions whenever it suited him or he wanted to. Like the player of the violin, he played me and I wanted to be played. I wanted him but he didn't even need me. I ached for him but somehow he had not even written my name on any part of himself. My strings were sore and yet the notes had not been practiced as yet. No pencil brushed its dark colour against my clean clear white page as yet. He was my father and I need to let him go. I need to focus on Noddy now.

Chapter 9

He plays with my emotions and I play like the soft violin and the repetition of my needs is the same as the deep cut throbbing aching of the played strings. He plays me, I play myself. I am the violin and he is the bow, my strings are red and sore and the deeper he rubs his bow up and down, the deeper the need. My throat swallows a thick ripe lump as I ask myself "Is this real life?"

Families came and some strayed, others never did, friends came in plentiful moods and each one of them brought their joys and delights and many conversations entangled with their webs of deceit and compassionate care and then there were all the rest. The fame game that Father played in all the time, that I have been here and before, that my own father struck the same cord again and again but then, it did not really affect me as I was the child. Now that I wear the adult shoes in this new life, I have had to grow up, mature overnight and be whatever Noddy wants me to be and whenever he wants. He is not cruel or unkind but just does not have any time for me, the real Me, the one who aches and lusts for him to come home, the aching begins to embed even deeper. We talk in a proper civil manner and he even sits next to me and yet, we can exchange words but not those with any heartfelt convictions.

Nights are meant for dreaming and fulfilling forbidden fruits, after all "oranges are definitely not the only fruits." They do have sweetness, bitterness, colour, juice and a thirst quenching appeal and then, there is the hard-nosed skin, tough and yet it comes very handy for all sorts. I suppose I should stop talking about myself. Day in, day out, I sit alone and yet it is wonderful when others are alive in my environment. A whole day often passes away as I sit with my open pen with no ink and the dried out diary in the other hand wanting to write and yet the page that is now to the new day is empty as another day goes by. How much shopping can I do? How much of going nowhere can I get used to and all this is ideal for those who yearn it, but as for me, I need a person who I can call my own, people who are actually living their life with me. I was under the illusion that a married life was to be shared and when I saw Zippy with her husband, Danny, who both spent quite a lot of time in our house, I was convinced that what I believed was right.

Father would often ponder before retiring for the night and whilst silently marching up and down the sitting room where we indulged with coffees in the evening, after a good few moments he would quietly clear his throat and then arch his brow and with great hesitation, he would then ask, "You are alright, aren't you? I mean everything is good in that department, right, between Noddy and yourself?" How could I even begin to explain my trivial anxieties or lack of faith or understanding about the coming of two people? How could I even try to find the appropriate words to say that apart from sharing the same house, the same family, the same bed, there is not much else that he seems to want to share!

I cannot explain because I cannot burden him with this and what exactly is this anyhow? On the surface everything is glorious and those are the words that Sunny's wife uses for Noddy and me. She thinks that we are a match made in heaven but then I have never been there and if I do ever go there, it will be with a one-way ticket only. This is how married life is, a one-way ticket until the day that you are sent your own personal ticket to accompany him upstairs.

I have tried all that possibly came into my head. I even indulged by watching the politics with them. I sat in the middle of the hub to be the center of Noddy's attraction and it's not as if he doesn't notice me, but it's as if I am one of the boys and to be honest, the only time he ever touches me is when the bed will hear the rumble tumble and then as I try to get more of him, he has already started to wither his tired eyes away from this wide-awake woman.

I am not a woman yet but Sunny's wife thinks that once married, every female becomes a woman. The rumbling of bodies made a girl into a woman. How strange because I thought you become a woman with age or when you give birth to something that you both have made together. In spite of certain actions, I have still not become a woman and I don't desire to have a child so to bridge that gap or to fill that emptiness by no means and I know that it will not bring us closer either, so really, I do not want to have something that I would love maternally but would love to have one if it brings us closer together. Maybe like my father and mother.... that didn't happen to them, so how can it happen for me?

I tried to become more involved in their work, the family business, but I was told that our woman only do house chores and so I wasn't allowed to go and work outside either and anyway, I don't even know what I would have done outside. Could I have been the girl who sells ice cream to those snooty-nosed kids whose noses are always dirty and their pockets with small change that's never enough to buy half of an ice cream, let alone a small one, but they have the tenacity to point with their half-bitten nailed finger at the picture of the biggest cone possible? Working outside, politics and a career and with that, even going to college is a boys' role in this society and maybe my own father's society as well. They are of the same generation, of the same stamina and of the same gentle-toned stubbornness. They are both kind but it is a slow killing way.

Months have passed, but Father and Kaka, born regulars and so were we all in my old house, but since being married, that old house somehow just seemed not like a closed book but as if I could not open the pages either. The pages of the new diary here in this new house are still so very new. If certain things were new in this new life then, how come the more that the pages of the diary were flicked over, the emptier I started to feel? At times, I would look at the recycling bin in the back yard and think how Sunny always spoke about conserving the environment and recycled everything he possibly could. Can we recycle life, no, so why bother with the contents? Life will all recycle and become nothing. Just like the one with the red, drip, drip, emptiness.

If I didn't know what "it", and I do mean "it", really is, then what could I explain to my own father or my husband's father now or even to Kaka or Sunny? The only other female in my life was Sunny's wife and she thought my life was perfect. What words of the alphabet could I possibly string together to spell out this thing? There was only one thing I did know and that was that the recycling bin would become empty one day, just like life. A whole year has gone by and even today I am sitting in our bedroom looking out of the window. The shutters are pulled way back against the flamed walls and I sit and swing gently on the big chair. Today is the day that I have to put Mother's veil back on my head as that night when we both rumbled for the first time, he took it off and told me that young beautiful fruits should not be covered because they need to be ripened naturally. That is what I have been doing for the whole year, getting ripe for life and for him and the galloping stallion within him.

The oranges had ripened over the year and though my skin was not zesty like the real fruit, it was always full of colour and strangely enough, it was even more colourful when I put the veil back on to my head. I chose the exact day of my wedding and whilst everyone was at work, I had carefully looked at all the veils on my head one-by-one rather than on the rails as before and around my neck and somehow, it had felt that maybe the girl had been ripened and the fruits had been naturally grown and were now ready to be picked. A year later, I was going back to the girl who through life had grown overnight into a woman and then I was subdued into marriage and I did have a lot of baggage. He made me forget who I really was and the baggage I was actually carrying. He played with my inner self and I could hear the violin strings gently simmering every day. Today of all days I realized that in fact nothing has changed or gotten better apart from the one thing that is the only constant reminder of my mother had been wedged apart from me and the saddest thing was, that it didn't actually tear me apart at all because I was empty a long time before that.

That day the men had come home together and I could hear that laughter before I could see their dusted feet enter the living room. They all looked once and then a few times more at my head and I could hear their questions coming out from underneath their breath. They sat and munched loudly whilst grinding away at their teeth with hollow rabbit leaves and hard-nosed orangey carrots. I watched and enjoyed their humour. They were such a great laugh to be around but he didn't make me really a part of him even though I was a part of them together. I was truly married to the whole family and I loved that, but I needed a bit more of him. I just needed that something that would bridge the gap between lunchtime and suppertime, from the time when the sun is trying to hide and the people look around for the sighting of the moon to guide them with some light.

"What's been happening today, dearest? What did you do to celebrate your wedding anniversary then?" Father gently simmered his warm words as he looked into the pain of my eyes and continued by asking if I was wearing the veil on my head to celebrate this day. Gently, I tried had to hide the pain but leave the emptiness quite visible as he uttered that little things should be celebrated.

I softly murmured that to celebrate my or rather our engagement, it would have had to have the two people to be at home to celebrate it together and he has been at work all day whereas I was at home all alone.

"Well, let's fix this right now. Noddy, get up and take your dearest wife out and go and enjoy yourselves and come back late if you want to make a real night of it. Don't forget to spoil her and treat her well, boy."

"Alright, I will." With that, his gaze offers a delightful smile and his eyes slowly peered slightly smaller with every second. He raised his eyebrows and then a small dimple gathered within his crease whilst sitting comfortably beside his lips. He put his hand out to me whilst I put my head down but silently, I dragged my feet into his direction. We both had eaten a little by now but there was always enough space in his stomach to put more in and as for me, well, I think some people just eat a lot whereas others simply don't have the appetite for that much of life.

That evening we serenaded the night park's bright lights, the streets so busily lit with people and none that we could say "hello" to and the ice cream van and the juice bars all flooded with swarms of people in this thirty-five degree temperature and even so, we just walked slowly past them. There was no Madonna or Lakeed or even Sultana here that my eyes could search for and I had no need to either, as today was a very beautiful day. It was the start of this new life once again and today, for once, he was with me, a year later, but with me and because he was with me, the veil had come off once again. He told me to take it off even before we set foot out of the door. It was as if it was a dream, him and that young bride or the married woman with the burdened shoulders, almost turning into her mother. I don't know which one of those was actually better.

The night stayed young and youthful and full of laughter like the moon and stars in the lit sky and so were our own eyes lit brightly amongst the darkness. We ate and drank lots of wine which I never did before. We walked the paths together that we never did tread and then we shared the chocolates that he brought, even though half of them fell to the floor and the flowers, all orange and yellow that he brought with me on his arm, they gently slithered their way out of the cheap plastic bag except for the one in his small pocket and mine in my hair.

The veil was nowhere to be seen and nor was that woman who started the day wearing it. We stumbled our way into the house whilst telling one another to keep quiet as we don't want anyone to hear us coming in at four o'clock in the morning. We straddled along the staircase and then slumped heavily onto our bed, together. It seemed so perfect and right and that could have been us together forever. There seemed to be some rumbling and tumbling but none that I could clearly remember and then as always that sun came to awaken our senses and as it slowly peered through the closed shutters with its eyes only half open, I opened mine to look at the clock on my side table. Wow, it had been light a very long time ago and yet I had only just realized. My head throbbed, my eyes ached and my whole body felt as if it had been rumbled a good few times.

I felt like nearing myself to him real closely but then I would be disturbing the silence. So instead, I opted to just watch the silent movement of his hair. Noddy looked so perfect but why can I not be his perfect picture, to keep? He has kept me for one year and a day now, but somehow these days seemed empty but a few, like an empty shoebox waiting for someone to own it or the still trampoline waiting for someone to liven it up or even the dusty violin who has been dying to be played. If I don't wake him up then I will never

218

need to know who once owned the empty shoebox or the "still" trampoline or even the reason why the violin is so dusty. It did not matter about the dust. I was the bow lying next to my Master and yet I wasn't broken.

I was still engrossed in him being there with me for such a long time that him getting up, bathing, getting ready and sitting to eat at the table were all golden moments. A year and a day over and when all the house had been emptied out like the empty larder or the pull-out squeaky empty cutlery drawer, today has become just like another day with the minus of yesterday as if, it had not even come and gone, an ordinary day in an ordinary life and the walls and the insides all empty. Even though the two workers were with me all day long and I was at home quite a lot, but I didn't have to be. I was free to go anywhere I wanted so long as I took the watchman and her with me. No one ever told me to be back at a certain time or not to go to a certain place. There were no restrictions but life itself.

Life itself wasn't going anywhere and once again I was alone and withered. It wasn't as if I didn't belong because indeed I did in this household and it wasn't even the fact that I had no on because it was far from the truth. So with all this on my side, why am I still alone? It is indescribable how I can hear a pin drop and yet no one actually is here to drop any and I do not sew, knit nor crochet. Silence is supposed to be golden but this is way beyond any colour, all the shades of colours are at the back of my head, so I have passed them and remember them still and they connect me to that place of happiness. Whoever she is, this happiness that is pulling me from the nest into the wild outdoors, from the sane into insanity and from the bare-headed girl into a veiled woman and even to that, not my own veils, so no protection from my own, but from someone else. From one head to another. From one's body heat to someone else's.

I can feel her body heat and I can feel my own. There is a difference in the textured heat. I can feel the bareness of my uncovered head and somehow I am not complete so quickly. I put Mother's red veil back onto my head. It's heavy and burdening and that is how I want to feel, protected by her in any way possible. Something almost empty is better than total emptiness like me. The razorblade was sharp and neatly kept in Noddy's shaving compartment and I tried really hard to fight this big fight and not even go near the cabinet at all but it was a battle that Mother had lost and a year and a day later, I have found myself in that same place. Different house, different people, same body and same heart.

Somehow I didn't even realize where my walk was taking me from the direction of the kitchen where we all had breakfast together. I wasn't alone there from the empty chairs and the food engraved plates and the knives and forks still perfectly polished and sparkling but the fingers full of tantalizing smells and then the girl inside was still hollow even though she had eaten. She had then felt a little empty so, she went to her bedroom and dug out her respect and honour which once belonged to her mother and guarded herself against it, in a hope that it may ward off evil but even that, didn't fill that hollow girl's heavy heart so, she slowly went to the bathroom cabinet where razors and blades were in their plenty mode.

One small incision to a small crack of the skin and it enfolded into more and more and this tender girl needed that, the woman felt the pleasure of the pain. Right now it was better to feel something rather than emptiness. Emptiness was lonely but feelings were real and strong so I had something. My eyes dripped as did my wrist and strange how I was unaware of the one feeling, was this me or her? This time was a real duplicate of her, her long hair dripping down like mine, arms now dangling down beside her and me and my tongue wrestling with unknown words that would not come out, the tongue safely within the mouth twirling around the elasticated words.

I could see her lying now with life quite still within her, her blood running ever so slowly like a creepy crawly and the clothes draped and her veil safely on her head. How respected we both looked, the world now turning around and it felt really good as I had never been on a musical roundabout at the fun fair. A merry-go-round. That means people are meant to be happy on this merry thing and my head feels happy. My droopy arms and legs feel exactly that and I can feel my ankles and wrists but nothing after that. I can feel her warmth, as she blows on my frowned brows with her cold breath and her dilated pupils, dark and dusty, stare with much openness into mine. She is trying to say something as I am trying to reply to her tender pressured words, hers and mine, but today she doesn't need to talk and me neither. Her hair, whiskey at the ends tickles my desired life as I open my fluttering eyes and see her clearly. There is no smile, no remorse for leaving me but she smiles as her eyes wander onto my veil. She is happy, she is happy, she is happy. I am happy, I am happy, yes, I am happy.

I couldn't hear her anymore but I could still feel her within my own belly button. I could feel the coldness of her cold touch still on my head and she is within my own eyes wearing exactly the same veil as I am wearing now. My short memory starts to tick away. I want to remember Father now, not the new father but my own father. I wonder how he is now. I have not seen him for a few months now as I neatly folded my own life away and without even a flutter of my eyelids, I embraced this new joyous life where I saw the young kid transform into that woman who embraced the veil honourably. The veil, it always had to be Mother's as it was the only way of keeping her close, very much within myself.

A year has lapsed since when? Since I got married or indeed way before that, since her own departure or since the veil found its new home. Home, well this is my new home but it feels like a house. It is my new house and my own real father's house was his home and my home was where Mother laid her own hat to rest, her mind and soul was where our home was. Home, quite strangely enough seems to be a very long way away and almost so far in the distance that I can smell the home and yet I cannot see it any longer. I can feel it within my own bones as I crunch my hands together and yet they are quite empty and my feet altogether. They are clean but they are so tainted and absorbed by the dust of that home, the fine eccles of soft earthy dust particles within my body moisture. My nostrils flare open and it feels as if I am once more in my old home, the smell of the trickling dew just outside of the front door and the newspaper crunch as Father folds it tightly underneath his armpit as he closely watches her move gallantly from the sink to the dining table, leaving behind the masked trail of her own flesh. She deliberately chooses to remain ignorant of his whims.

I too wish I could be ignorant but instead it has been the other way round and then as I no longer feel that I am the Master and keeper of my womanly self, I feel a strong presence around me of the one whose skin I can still recollect through all the bodily hair. I can feel his footsteps underneath my own feet as if I have trodden on them myself. Suddenly the door is now ajar but my eyes have already become far too heavy for me to even recognize his whereabouts and yet I can see him from the back of my eyes, his heavy hands clamp my delicate body and all I can sense is his heaviness and his sweaty body heave.

I don't know if I am here or not, how or who else has come here and then I can feel his voice vibrating some silent words within my eardrums and my lifeless dampened arm being held tightly into his masculinity and a tight clasped pressure is forced on my seeping wrists like the thirsty cat to its plate of milk. I can feel the cut and the pain entices me. I hiss. It seems quite wonderful as it is better to have some emotion rather than none, better to have pain than not to feel anything and to have him close to me in a freaky way rather than there be some distance between us. At least he is here with me, I have no more complaints. Even now the only words that mean anything or indeed make any real sense is that the wondering of the fact that is the veil still on my head? I can feel my hand on the veiled head and then I can feel the twitch of my curved lips. "Mother, my mother, my mother's veil."

Dignity, respect and the veil. Her veil's not just hanging within her own tongue or being released like the running tap and certainly not hidden away like the masks that never get worn and yet kept nurtured behind the wooden planks of wood. No, I had to make them a part of the real world as I know it and as I live it. It is the only way to keep her alive even if I have to suffer in the process and really he should, have kept her alive and with my eyes fully shut now, I ask that question within my heart. Why didn't he keep her alive within himself, for himself and for me and I do not believe that he could not have done that? He could do everything but the one thing that we both females needed to be done, to keep us alive, he didn't do.

She was the thread on the reel, the water that freely flows, the river with no means and the soul that never did get set free, trapped within the freedom. I am the thread that is spun around her reel. I am the water that saw her precious young life freely flow away. We both are rivers that needed to reach the mouth and we were free until the time when the veil trapped us within. My life trapped my mother's veil and her life trapped by her honour and dignity and his respect. "Respect" was the word that was hidden between the poet's unfulfilled desires and the woman's inability to write any chosen words on paper. Both of them were slaves to their own calamities and I was also part of this, totally unaware at first but slowly the yearning and the wanted of the silent words and unsaid tears seeped through the empty lines to write a destiny.

I can feel someone carrying me and my light weight stretched out onto their manly arms with no burden but, there seemed to be panic stricken words that didn't make sense, body odours that I could not smell anymore and voices that did not make sense and I could feel under the dripping sweat, laid layer of soft bedding that cradled me. I try to flicker my eyes as they felt tight against my skin, the salty tears have glazed them to tell another tale. Tales are the only things that are left in this woman's world, the only particle of her remain in her tale of who and what she is!

Chapter 10

Who was I? I am Meera and I am the wife of Veer
Noddy Singh and the daughter of Shere and Rani
Chaudhrey. Veer Noddy Singh re-lit the flame of
love that day when he found me just the same way
as I found Mother that day. I didn't know what to
do with her but he knew how to save me. I wasn't
able to call anyone to help this helpless young
vulnerable child Meera and so that became the
curse of Meera, to hold onto and live with. The
death of Rani Chaudhrey in the hands of her own
daughter, who in spite of the fact that she knew all,
she chose to ignore it and wish for it all to go
away. She let her die, so it's her fault and she
deserves the same.

Noddy saved me, through his breath, through
his quick thinking and most of all, his love. He
cradled the person within me and laid me on the
bed, called the doctor and stayed and stayed until I
was well enough, not just physically as that was
soon enough, but mentally. He knew the answers
that I had the questions to and he knew what the
words on my lips were, way before my tongue
would release them. Three long days in my
bedroom to recover psychologically, to get my
own head to think of "Who am I?" I did know
"who I am" as I know that here was this woman
strong enough to take on the world except she had
lost certain bits of the puzzle along the way. She
didn't know where to start looking, in spite of the

fact that it was staring me in the face every day.

Within these three days, Father spent so much of his valuable time sitting and playing chess with me, especially when Noddy did have to go out and it felt almost complete as if this father was indeed my second father. He showered me with so much love, always kissing me on my forehead, talking and sharing parts of his personal life with me, but then how could I not have seen this all before? Was I in another space where I could not be reached? Noddy spent most of this time sitting, talking and sharing tender moments even though the moments when I was continuously asking, why he had changed.

His answer was always that he felt that I wanted my space and felt that I was always keeping my distance, maybe needed time to get over losing my Ma and then there was me, who felt that too. He said that he had thought that maybe I needed time and that time heals and so was hoping that my mind and soul would heal in its own time. A year had gone by, her veil was strongly tying us both together and my punishment was handed out. A child denied to see her mother for the last time, see her suffer under the heat of the sun when in fact, I should have suffered and then she laid in that time to remind me of her every day and how she suffered and how I allowed it all and did nothing. So I did have to pay, so I did take it off at times. I had to be punished for it and so that is what I deserved and got.

Even though I was and had been asleep for the

best part of that afternoon, all evening and that night as well, but within, I was very much alive from the soul and the only thing that was important was to die with dignity by dying with Mother's veil on my head, a respected wife and daughter, no sister or mother to anyone and my mouth could hear only five words being repeated, "'til death do us part", the veil is the only thing that is mine to leave behind. There could be parting of her and me. I did not want a parting of a mother and her daughter. I was the girl who lived in that big bubble and I did not want it to pop.

The bubble did pop as my blood dripped slowly down my fair skin and it painted the baby fine thin hair along the way and then, the following day, I did wake up to reality and it was as if I was let out of that bubble after such a long time, over a year ago, but I could smell her and without saying anything to anyone or looking at anyone. My eyes searched for her veil, the one I had on yesterday. I know it was the next day as the clock with the smiley face forever told the day, the month, the year and of course the time. I saw it, my honour, thrown like junk and I wanted someone to pass it to me, to cover me up.

"No, no more Meera, no more of this. You are a girl, not a woman. Live like a young girl. There is no need for formalities whatsoever," Father's firm authoritative words meant what they uttered. I did not reply back. I was ordered to have some breakfast in bed and that is exactly what I did do and then they all left the room except for Noddy, who told me to get up and get ready. In a soft murmur, just like the soft beating of my heart, I asked "Why?" He did not reply but instead he got my clothes out, something very young and colourful and full of life, that I have not even worn yet and he laid them onto the bed. There seemed to be so much life in those dead clothes, separated out to spread life.

There were so many question marks in my head and in my heart and I dare not ask, so instead I get ready and whilst doing so, I noticed the big white clean bandage around my wrist. It was not red, it was all clean. He watched my every move and told me to sit at the dresser and get ready. "Ready?" I asked. "Ready as a young girl should be," he muttered. He started brushing the ridges out of my hair and then he gently combed everything back. With his firm hand, he pushed the hair at the top of my head and we both watched the tossled parting take its natural shape. We both smiled.

"You know, Meera, that is the way I saw you the first time, but now there are a couple of things still missing. You apply the make-up for a young girl and I will find earrings for you and of course your wedding band that you never have worn as yet. I stare into the mirror and I see a girl who was young and tender with no streaks of life on her face and as I open my half-lit eyes, I see the woman with the wooden smile firmly placed and the swinging chair rocks merrily with her but then my own bottom sits firmly on the stool.

I can hear the paperboy with the dirty

fingernails scratching against his dirt and sweat from his palms to the nails paddling along with his six-toed feet and shouting all the while. His hands have more action than his tongue and the only action that he doesn't want is the mother sitting with her flat feet firmly on the gravely floor and her shriveled up hands showing the coarse life that she has endured and as with every day, she sits on her pride and wishes, and hopes that today, life may just bring a local well-wisher to her dwelling who may leave her some of his left-over's. She sits silently stirring the metal pot with the fresh water from the well; slowly the wood drags the water along its empty journey. It's just as well that he has helped himself to lots of freebie food and the left-overs that others have slung in the paper bags. He thanks him upstairs that at least he doesn't have to waste money on his hunger. How do I know him or them and who are they really?

My stomach churns itself around almost like the dryer, heated and tired but I crave no food like those outside, the outside people. The outside people. Wow! Yes, they are the outside people and I have not thought of them for over a year? We were all not important to each other. Her chair rocks and I feel mine with my feet. It is so very still. "Why are you sitting there so still? Come on, chop chop, get ready. Here, I've bought you a cup of tea. Sip this sugary Indian delight whilst applying your make-up.

He stands like a bodyguard and I do as I am told, no not told, asked, it's different. "Are those people really the outside people and us the inside people?" I hesitantly mutter.

His forehead dimples like the hard curved chisel and in an instant he softly replies, "Outside people and inside people, aren't we all just people?"

"Yes, but, but you see we all live indoors and they live outdoors. We are trapped in here behind these walls that tell so many fables and then them outside, well, they tell tales from their own mouths."

"And?" he replies. With this, I am silent. He continued, "Meera, we are all the same. You are free to go out and it's only because of safety that someone accompanies you and it was the same for my mother and most other women as well, as we live in a culture where men still feel we have to protect our women, that's all, Meera."

Slowly, he wipes the sweat from his brow but there is no sweat of any kind on me. His finger drips the same way as she did and for the first time in a long time, I realize that things that drip are not all bad and then the only thing that I can remember is the dripping of my own tears, slowly and with speed, loudly and in silence, two eyes and then four eyes, but not one body alone, two in harmony. Until the monsoon rains have dried in the heated blue sky and suddenly the sun has come out and it has been ages, since the sun hasn't been seen through my eyes. I can hear the birds singing and flocking their flappers loudly outside and the ever so busy cars filling the street outside with the joy and laughter of the kids outside and toddlers

232

screaming with laughter. Laughter, I haven't heard that in a very long while. I run to the window and stare.

"Noddy, please come and have a look outside. It's as if everyone and everything has come back to me and in my life, like, like when?"

"Like when your mother was still alive, that's when."

The politics penny had truly dropped into the opening of the feel-good factor machine where everyone is rewarded with delights. We stood side-by-side, hand-in-hand, arms touching one another's and the stream of blood flowing through our veins. I could feel him almost as if it was all going through my own body, as if life was once again awoken in my own insides almost as if the Duracell battery had restarted the ticking again. He continued his persuasions. He swayed his head as I nodded many times, his hands showed what his words lacked in whilst my eyes flickered at the sights that actually made sense.

I sat on the big swinging chair once again and yet it did not swing and how I was so sure it did swing exactly like that day and in the same manner, for her as well? She should be here and I should be me. There are two of us, one is dead as the other is still very much alive. I have not felt alive for a very long time, simply being alive and actually living are two different things but I have been living, though it wasn't freely but more than that I was punishing myself and denying myself the right to be free and happy. How can I or anyone actually forget how to live and be alive? I don't know how from being alive I simply went on to live and how a good part of me, especially the part that has life in it, suddenly or gradually die with that blood that didn't move anymore.

We talked and talked until our mouths ran dry just like the mouth of the dried up river and our tongues felt like twigs on a hot summer's day. We revisited the time when only a few hours ago, I sat at the dressing table to apply my make-up and Noddy was going to choose the jewellery. We brushed our hair and gently I took the comb and placed it carefully into the bin beside me. It doesn't belong in my life anymore. I am going to lay it to rest. It was as if it was all me but two different worlds. One world where I was a carefree young girl where Mother and her veil were the normal way of life and everything in it was, well, normal. Then something just happened that I did not contemplate, understand or even think about with her in that position and me, in that circumstance, and the pain had gotten the better of me because all I could think or feel was, pain. It had become my best friend. So what I lost, I gained in another way but little did I realize I would need to pay the price at some point.

The politician's jigsaw puzzle in my own head consisted of many pieces, where if I had lost only one tiny piece, the rest would not and could not make sense. In my case, I did not even know how many pieces were lost or troubled, big or small and I know that even if there is only a small current in the sea's wave, it can trouble all that follows thereafter. I felt as if every time I opened my eyes, in spite of the fact of what I was looking at, everything beyond what my eyes did visualize, there was the biggest burden of all. The evenings drew closer and beyond the live bodies of Father, Kaka and many others, the thing I saw first was always the darkness at the back, the black hole that was always making a home within me every evening and at night, when in fact I should have been dead to the world. I could see clearly the black darkness twirling powerfully and loudly like the turbines of the aeroplane engines.

When mornings did finally arrive, I was relieved as I thought that my pain may not get the better of me on this and every new day, but alas, as I saw them and her at all times and continuously and she uttered absolutely no words but her silence and I understood that so well. Her eyes, hollow and empty as I had seen them, disheartened with me as I could not save her and even through her and everyone else, I saw the forest and its danger and darkness and its hidden mystery. It wasn't just out there; it was real and within me. A young girl had not crawled out from the black hole as yet and then, I get entered into yet another one. I do not have the know-how or even a slight inclination.

The hair did not get brushed nor combed, the colours were worn with more willingness and there was no more hiding away from happiness. For the first time in ages, I did not feel guilty about looking forward rather than back. The veil and now, it was my own and draped around my neck, a little on the shoulder. It was mine and it felt good. It belonged to me, not the past. He chose my earrings, necklace and the wedding band that was supposedly mine but never did find its way onto my finger in over a year and hey, could this be the coke can ring? I observed its shine and glamour and then I saw our initials separated by a tiny heart. Yes, this ring does celebrate our life together. Finally, I applied the thick lipstick, dark, dangerous and dusky, but at the moment it was too early to accept. Quietly, I take out a wet wipe and I see a vision in the girl in the mirror's eyes. She opens her hand and let's go of a precious teardrop.

Glossy baby pink, it suits me a whole lot more and this is me, with my vision, my own identity, my own Me. I am still trying to find the real Me, but it is like finding the dew amongst the midst, the splinter amongst the wood or the one that my mother used, a needle in a haystack and as my father would always say, sometimes people try and get oil out of a stone, but the search continues. The search for what exactly, the things that should not be mystery really, the family of politicians? My own father's greed for the politicians' policies to come out into the powerful world. My own mother falling into the voters' trap. What is right and what is wrong?

Rights and wrongs needs and demands, the greed to succeed and the greed to yearn. The place of power and the power to keep hold of, their silent and still fight continued forever not just on the surface in front of me and yet never in front of others, for we had and even now in this house, have a very disciplined household. Tangles can be aired once the cracks of the heavy wooden doors are smoothed over but not necessarily with the key turned and loud voices rarely heard as stern looks had much more to say than the words themselves. Sometimes silence can say so much that words would never be able to entangle themselves in a proper manner.

Power is politics and politics is life and that is the way our life was and is now because we grew up in that orderly manner where the men went out to work and the women did remain "ladies of leisure". Noddy said that if I wanted to go and study or find work or indeed work with the family that is all fine because whatever makes our lives work is fine with father and him. Forever, my father rules our house, my mother ruled me and now in this house, Father rules the political game and Noddy is stepping exactly in his father's shoes. They even wear the same-sized shoe or is it not really like that? I stare at his back now as I can see his mood through his thin cotton shirt. It shivers slightly and I can see his hidden pain but he is a man who cannot show his grief the way women can. None of these men can or is that what I think.

We moved ourselves downstairs and Father surprisingly sat in his usual seat, calm and collective and even his gestures are like a politician, the ones who are always on the television, waving their hands around to express what their words cannot convince. Their body language shows how they will flicker here and there to avoid the uncomfortable questioning or answering or the avoidance of the truth. He is genuinely a nice guy but then so is my own father. What connection is there between the politics and us the people and what is the connection between the politicians and the veil or all those who are driven to wear them, and furthermore, who sits in the driving seat and drives the mechanics of the family dynamics forward?

Can a cold metal vehicle drive a live human to do what they or she does not want to do or is the mother wearing the veil herself and will she insist or embed the rule to wear it into her daughter's young manipulative mind or is she finding her inner self and the real woman in and outside of herself? Father gets up and wishes me well whilst patting me on the back with a chunky big hug. He has hugged me so many times and yet his embrace has never ever felt so good as today. My inner self felt so soothed and is that because he needed to be soothed? Did he lay blame upon himself or did he feel sorry for me?

I leave my own house now and it's really strange because it actually does feel like my own today for the first time ever but it was almost as if it was not the last time here for me but indeed I was coming back, maybe a better person. Where was I going and why I just don't know except that I am being led by Noddy? We leave and as he closes the door behind us, I take a deep breath and all I can smell is not yesterday's kippers or even omelets, not Father and his heavy cigar breath or the aromatic smells of the lingering white linen sprays or even Noddy who awaits with me, side-by-side, but I do smell my own bodily smell, not of my perfume or flowered clothes or of the lipstick I am wearing but definitely of my own self.

It felt as if I had cleaned my smelling senses after such a long time, but how could that have been true? We enter the grand Range Rover and the driver is already sitting with his smirky wide smile, lips licked to a glossy seal and his hat firmly stuck on his head. I take the seat behind the driver and I don't move over as I know that Noddy may or may not sit with me as I am unsure. We have not had many moments like this often. He leans his face towards the driver and tells him that his services are not needed today. He puts his smile away and takes his hat off. Quietly, he moves from the seat and heads off into the air.

Noddy winks at me and arches his left brow in the direction of the front passenger seat. I obey. We sit side-by-side. He holds my hand. I feel delighted like the kid who had just brought some sweets. He starts the engine and I can smell the leather warmed up by my own heat. It resembles the same smell as the polish that gets cradled onto the furniture daily and yet today I could relate to it, only today. There is this thick fog that seems to be living in silence within me and just now when I heard the engine spark from this car, somehow it felt as if its exhaust pushed a small particle of it away from within. My head feels a little bit lighter now.

We listen to the stereo and CD that boar out some wonderful songs and I was so enticed by the tranquility of it that I quickly forgot my own demons. Noddy got out and came round to get me out and then in sheer silence we walked, hand-in-hand, to the front door which as always was ajar. Kaka stood just inside of that and my own father just behind him. There was no one else and yet my eyes searched for someone but even I didn't know who? I searched and searched and my eyes were bewildered as they were longing to see that someone who they had yearned for, but apart from a new cleaner and the gardener, the rest of the house stood still and alone.

If I am feeling like this with all these people around me and yet alone, lonesome and isolated, then how do all the dwellers in this house feel? We all kissed, hugged and let some well-kept tears be released and as I left the arms of Father, I looked around. It smelt of emptiness and tainted smells of her remains. Everything looked as it was before and I could tell that Father had lost a little weight but Kaka has gained the extra pounds that Father lost. Some eat more in emptiness as others find their appetite for life diminishes. Time had healed the cracked heels on the floor but the hearts within were still fragile. Quickly, I raced like a mad woman around the house looking for traces of life but alas the girl was right here right now. She was not within us three still but her memories were alive and kicking and would remain so.

Without even thinking of my own whereabouts, I found myself in their bedroom, the wardrobe perfectly lined with his and her clothes, her veils surrounded her suits and saris perfectly. I put my dampened cheeks to the clothes. I think that they will forever smell dusky. All of her filled everything in here including the dead and alive. The swinging chair, her swinging chair laid decorated for her return and it overlooks the open big window which is full of freshness and tales of the outside people seen through the open eyes of the inside people. I can see them both idly swinging in harmony, unaware that I was watching them through the crack of the frame whilst they teased and tainted. There were echoes of sniggering and then bouts of happy laughter as her lashes touched his moustache, as I watched his fingers stroke her hair, she tilts her head. I flutter my eyelids and now the chair is empty and I feel lost once again but then I can smell Noddy and feel his tight clutch on my index finger. I am not alone or isolated, I have family.

We roam her whereabouts and explore her existence and end up in the exact position of her last phase, the bit which I missed, the ritual of cleansing and then we walk her farewell journey to the outside where she was burnt into nothing. There is no trace of her here anymore, no ash, no dirt, no nothing. Here there lays yellow flowers of crops, vibrant and young. In similar strides, we

241

follow the route that her urn travelled. It lay in the exact position as I was. Noddy and I both grab its golden value, and my father joins us with her red and gold threaded veil and places it over it. We all get into my father's car, Noddy, Father and I and my mother in my lap sit together whilst Kaka drives us. He hums along just as he always has and then he parks the vehicle alongside the perfect flows of our own river, perfectly clean, slow flowing and still bearing the brunt of all its population.

We all circle its width and then in the corner where the water lilies beautify the water with their full glory, we place the urn to swim its way to the heavens, not above, but right here, right now, in-between the seas of our own eyes, we watched her serenity and poise as she dipped and rose and as we prayed for her goodbye. We set her free from her dusky world, from us and her worldly responsibilities and asked her to release us from her captivity and forgive our sins. The veil, her veil, Mother's veil set sail on the respected urn as the layers spread their wings to honour her pride and dignity. My father's chest breathed in the crispy air as he released a melodious sigh without any entangled words. Kaka's damp lashes tilted and lifted in his heavy cloud whilst Noddy and I stood tall, proud to be standing together without isolation and proud to have one another.

My mother's veil was finally set free along with Mother. She left us for the final time and went off to make her new home with him upstairs, and she

242

believed that we do and have to go to him at some point with a one-way ticket and non-refundable. After setting her free, we, all four of us, felt that it truly was time to move on. "Move on" was the way forward and it was all good as we moved away from the nearby river and came back to my father's and we all had dinner, served by the new lady. Kaka and I sat and talked. Noddy and I and Kaka all sat and talked as never before and then whilst having coffee, Father joined us on the way back from his political canvassing with his politician wheeler and dealer friends. My father, Kaka and I and Noddy all sat as never before to turn a new leaf.

New leaves, new lives and old ways never to return. Maybe that was what was indeed needed, time to iron out things that were badly creased and look forward and not back. That time had never returned again and maybe I just needed time to grieve step-by-step which I did revisiting and retracing my roots. It helped and I think that I did not have that time with her to grieve or with my father and because I had time to retrace and draw my own lines along the tracings of her final farewell, the farewell that I had no knowledge of. This day, this moment gave me time to accept my pain, grief and acceptance of my mother, her veil, her life full of respect, honour, a woman's role in society and society itself. The veil, the politics, my old and new family and the religion and culture of our society.

I think that I had slowly put my feet into my

243

own mother's shoes and hopefully now I have learnt to wear my own. Maybe one day, I too will have a daughter, who will grow up into an individual and not into me. But for now, I have a son and he too will move along with his father and grandfather and now that another year has gone by and a son has fallen into my lap, Noddy's pride and joy, and I am waiting for a girl to accompany me sometime soon. There will be remembrance but no veils of dominance or captivity and there are no inside and outside people. Somehow these groups have become one where different people have a separate role to play in life, to get by. As with the main bloodline in our lives, there are players who play the politics game, others who just live with them and most who simply know that a thumbprint or cross makes them more powerful than the rest.

The veils have combined in harmony with Mother's and mine and now there is not much of a difference, hers or mine, it's almost the same. There is Marilyn Monroe and of course Madonna at times but now we have an understanding of love and respect, whereby I don't change her and she accepts me for who I am. I don't have to see the dark tunnel where the politicians dominate the light; they live with the non-conformers. They are just doing their job, like we women are and so are those on the outside. The veils don't have to conform to any female and yes, I do work with Noddy part-time and even went to study for a while. We are free to choose even though we could not choose our gender and where we are and when we would inhabit ourselves, but we can decide to believe if the grass is greener here rather than just the outside and elsewhere.